"I usually like

"Such as?" Noah asked.

Lily shrugged. "Zip-lining, sushi—"

"Wait a minute." He held up a hand. "You'll eat raw fish that could have who knows what in it, but you're afraid to get on a horse?"

At least she had the decency to look embarrassed. "I know it sounds silly—"

"Oh, it sounds more than just silly."

She was quiet for a moment. Then, "What would be truly silly, though, is to tell my children the truth when I haven't even made the effort to overcome my fear." She looked him in the eye. "If you're still willing to help me, I'm ready to accept your help."

His smile was instantaneous. "Then I'll see you Monday morning."

Standing there in the shade of an aspen tree, he searched her pretty face, feeling his heart swell with something that hadn't been there in a long time. Respect? The thrill of a challenge? Or something else he was too afraid to name?

It took **Mindy Obenhaus** forty years to figure out what she wanted to do when she grew up. But once God called her to write, she never looked back. She's passionate about touching readers with biblical truths in an entertaining, and sometimes adventurous, manner. Mindy lives in Texas with her husband and kids. When she's not writing, she enjoys cooking and spending time with her grandchildren. Find more at mindyobenhaus.com.

Books by Mindy Obenhaus

Love Inspired

Rocky Mountain Heroes

Their Ranch Reunion
The Deputy's Holiday Family
Her Colorado Cowboy

The Doctor's Family Reunion
Rescuing the Texan's Heart
A Father's Second Chance
Falling for the Hometown Hero

Visit the Author Profile page at Harlequin.com.

Her Colorado
Cowboy

Mindy Obenhaus

Recycling programs
for this product may
not exist in your area.

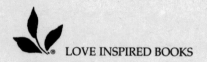 LOVE INSPIRED BOOKS

ISBN-13: 978-1-335-47911-2

Her Colorado Cowboy

Copyright © 2019 by Melinda Obenhaus

www.Harlequin.com

Printed in U.S.A.

Weeping may endure for a night,
but joy cometh in the morning.
—*Psalms* 30:5

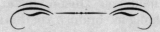

For Your glory, Lord.

Acknowledgments

Thank you, Allison Wilson,
for helping me brainstorm this story
and find the outcome it deserved.

Many thanks to Steve Wicke
for sharing your roping expertise.

Betty Wolfe, you're one of my favorite residents
of Ouray. Thank you for all your help.

To my loving husband, Richard,
where would I be without you?

Chapter One

Lily Davis had lost her mind.

She loathed horses. Yet, somehow, she'd allowed her children to talk her into taking them horseback riding. What was she thinking?

Knuckles white, she guided her luxury SUV across the cattle guard of Abundant Blessings Ranch and Trail Rides, her gaze darting from the majestic mountains that backdropped the picturesque setting to the menacing red-and-white metal building that sat a short distance from the road.

She swallowed hard. Any other time she would have put her foot down, but she was desperate. They'd only been in Ouray for three days, and already her kids were begging to go back to their friends and electronic devices in Denver.

Okay, so it was her ten-year-old son, Colton, who did most of the complaining. He thought everything was boring. On the contrary, her seven-year-old daughter, Piper, had proclaimed Ouray, Colorado, the most beautiful place ever. Which was good, because returning to Denver before the end of the summer was not an option. Not if she wanted to save her son from following in his father's footsteps.

She eyed her firstborn in the rearview mirror. With his sandy brown hair and green eyes, he favored her, though his blatant lies were a hallmark of his father. Something Lily found increasingly disconcerting. But learning of how he'd bullied another boy at school had spurred her into action. Because despite what Wade Davis might believe, the fact that they had money did not make them better than anyone else.

He'd agreed to let her take the kids away for the entire summer, instead of splitting the time the way they usually did. Whatever deal he was working must be big. She could only pray he wouldn't change his mind before August 15, the date they'd agreed upon for the kids' return.

Easing to a stop between another SUV and a sedan, she shifted into Park. Why couldn't they have just gone on another Jeep tour?

The kids were out of the vehicle before Lily even turned off the engine.

"Hurry up, Mommy." Piper's excitement had her blonder-than-blond ponytail swishing to and fro. The perpetually cheerful child had always been eager to try new things. A trait Lily usually admired. Until she suggested horseback riding.

Too bad Lily hadn't had the guts to say no.

Setting her booted feet onto the gravel, she rubbed her arms, eyeing the two chestnut-colored horses staring at her from the adjacent paddock. Did they know? Were they able to sense that another horse had once gotten the best of her?

"Aww…" Piper noted the pair. "Aren't they cute?"

Lily cleared her throat. "Horses are some of God's most beautiful creatures." Not to mention frightening. Her kids didn't see it that way, though, so she wasn't about to pass her fears on to them.

She drew in a deep breath, the once-familiar odor of horse and hay tightening her stomach. How was she ever going to pull this off?

"This is boring." Colton shuffled toward the entrance. "I want to ride them, not look at them."

Lily's gaze lifted to the mid-June sky. *God, please help me.* She glanced at her son. *In every way.*

Inside, the walls of the small but tidy lobby were lined with rustic wood planks. A couple with two boys who looked to be a little older than Colton sat on an old wooden church pew that hugged one wall.

"Mommy, look." Piper pointed above the doorway of what appeared to be an office. "A horseshoe."

"It's a horse barn." Arms crossed, Colton rolled his eyes. "They probably have, like, a million of those things."

"I don't care, Colton." Hands on her hips, his sister glared at him. "I still like them."

Before Lily could intervene, the sound of footsteps on concrete drew their attention.

She turned, feeling as though she'd suddenly stepped into a country music video. From his boots and Wranglers to the shiny belt buckle and straw Stetson perched on his head, this guy was all cowboy.

He stopped to address the other family. "If you all will head straight down this corridor—" he pointed to the long aisle behind him "—and to the right, Amber and Jackie are waiting with your horses."

As the group departed, he turned his attention to Lily and her children. "Welcome to Abundant Blessings Ranch." Tall and clean shaven, he tipped his hat back just enough to reveal dark brown hair and even darker eyes, like a rich espresso. He was older than she would have expected. Perhaps even older than her thirty-eight years, but not by much. And while his smile was pleasant enough, it did little to put her at ease. "I'm Noah Stephens. How can I help you folks today?"

Pressing one hand against her stomach, she fingered the silver chain around her neck with the other. "Um—"

"We want to ride horses." Piper stared up at the man, looking very matter-of-fact.

"You do?" His smile grew wider, forming creases around his eyes. "Well, I guess you've come to the right place then." He reached for one of a series of clipboards that hung on the wall. "I'll just need your mother to sign these papers." He handed the clipboard to her, along with a pen.

The knot in Lily's stomach grew even bigger as she filled in the required information. Why was she putting herself through this? She should have simply said no in the first place.

But then Colton and Piper would have wanted to know why. She couldn't bear the thought of telling them she was afraid. After all, she was their mother. The one who was supposed to be strong. And she was, most of the time. Right about now, though, she felt like that four-year-old girl who'd just been bucked off her first, and last, horse.

"How much riding have you kids done?" The cowboy looked from Colton to Piper.

"I've never been on a horse." Piper's blue eyes sparkled. "But I can't wait."

"That's good to know, because I want to make sure I pair each of you with the correct horse for your level of experience."

"What does it matter?" Colton shrugged. "It's just a stupid horse."

The cowboy straightened to his full six-foot-plus height, and Lily froze. What would he do? Everyone knew cowboys didn't tolerate disrespect. And her son had plenty. Would he tell them they couldn't ride?

Wishful thinking on her part.

Arms crossed, the man stared down at Colton, his expression stern. "Actually, horses are quite smart." His deep voice left no room for question. "And they're able to sense what kind of people are riding them." His gaze narrowed. "So you might want to keep that in mind, young man."

Under different circumstances, Lily might have chuckled. But by the time she handed the completed paperwork back to the cowboy, her stomach was churning.

His brow lifted. "Are you all right, ma'am?"

"Yes." However, the more she tried to psych herself up for this endeavor, the worse things became.

She grabbed a white-water rafting brochure from the rack against the wall and fanned herself, wondering when it had gotten so warm. All the while, the tossing and turning in her belly intensified.

This was not good. Not good at—

Just as the cowboy turned to talk with Colton and Piper, Lily bolted out the door. She rushed to the side of the building, her stomach in full revolt. Not once, but twice.

Standing there, doubled over, she heard someone behind her. *Oh, no. God please don't let it be—*

"You look like you could use a little help." That deep voice definitely didn't belong to Colton or Piper.

Mortified, she glanced at the cowboy and managed to eke out, "Don't let my children see me," before hurling again.

When she finally collected herself a short time later, she leaned against the metal building, feeling more than a little embarrassed. And all over the mere thought of riding a horse. She wiped her mouth, praying she wouldn't have a repeat performance.

Returning to the stable, she spotted Piper and Colton

halfway down the wide corridor that ran between a small arena and some horse stalls.

"Where were you?" Colton eyed her suspiciously.

"I had something I had to take care of." She forced a smile, hoping she didn't look as pale as she felt.

Fortunately, the cowboy reappeared with two horses before her son could ask any more questions.

It pleased her that one of them was nothing more than a Shetland pony, and she wondered if they might have another for her.

The man stopped in front of them, looking far too serious. "We have a slight problem."

Oh, no. Her kids were so looking forward to this, and now they weren't going to be able to ride. All because of her. Her silly fear had blown it for all of them.

The cowboy continued, "We had another family that arrived just before you. Typically, we prefer not to have any more than six guests on a trail ride. With you three, that would be seven."

Piper's bottom lip pooched out. "You mean we don't get to ride?"

"Man, we finally get to do something cool…" Colton kicked at clump of hay.

Lily's stomach tightened again. If only she hadn't panicked. Now she'd ruined everything.

"Of course," the cowboy finally said, "if one of you would be willing to stay behind, the other two could still go."

Lily jerked her gaze to his.

His dark eyes were directed right at her.

He was giving her an out. But why? Was he afraid she'd get sick again while they were on the trail? Or did he know she was afraid?

"I'm not staying," said Colton.

"If Colton doesn't hafta stay, I don't want to, either." Arms crossed, Piper peered up at Lily.

Looked like it was up to her to take one for the team. Something she was more than okay with this time. Thanks to Noah Stephens. However, it presented her with a new problem.

Mr. Stephens was a stranger. Colton and Piper were her greatest blessings. A gift from God she cherished with every fiber of her being. Could she trust this cowboy with her children?

Clearing her throat, she looked at her kids. Saw the disappointment etched on their faces. "I wouldn't want the two of you to miss out, either." She eyed the cowboy. He looked responsible. And he'd already shown he wasn't the type to stand for Colton's shenanigans. "Would it be all right if they went without me?"

He nodded. "So long as you signed the consent forms."

She looked at her children. "Are you two okay with that, or would you prefer to wait until later when we can go together?" Not that she'd be any more enthusiastic, but she'd settle for less nauseous.

"I can watch Piper," offered Colton.

"Yeah, Colton can watch me."

Lily couldn't help but laugh. For once her children were in agreement. "Okay. But I want you to be on your best behavior."

"We will," they said in unison.

The cowboy tipped his straw hat in her direction. "I promise to take good care of them."

To her surprise, she actually believed him. Probably because he'd come to check on her when she was outside. Something she found very chivalrous. And as they walked away, she couldn't help wondering what it would be like to be taken care of by someone like that. Someone strong, caring… Not self-serving like her ex.

She quickly shook away the thought. God and her children were her only priorities. Not love or any notions thereof. Especially with a cowboy.

"Mom, you should have seen it." Colton met his mother in the lobby, his enthusiasm obvious. And that made Noah happy.

The kid was far too young to have the kind of attitude Noah had witnessed prior to their ride. Angry. Disrespectful. The type of kid Noah hoped to help. Not that troubled kids were the focus of his soon-to-open rodeo school at Abundant Blessings Ranch. Still, Noah knew firsthand the difference horses could make in the lives of troubled kids and adults dealing with loss. They're what helped him get past the deaths of his wife and unborn child. And he had a feeling the root of Colton's anger had to do with some sort of loss, too. During their ride, the kid had mentioned that his parents were divorced. Was his father involved in his life?

While Noah's parents had loved each other until his mother succumbed to cancer three years ago, he'd had many friends whose lives had been impacted by divorce. He understood the pain and anger that came from such an experience. Especially when it was something they hadn't chosen and there was nothing they could do to fix it.

If only he could help those kids deal with their feelings by giving them a way to channel their emotions into something else. Or perhaps the kids would simply benefit from spending time with a good listener. He knew for a fact that horses were very good listeners.

"We got to ride on the mountain," Piper said.

Cute kid. Happy, smart, energetic… If his child had been a girl, he'd have hoped she'd be like Piper.

"Can I get a soda?" Colton watched his mother hopefully. "Noah said there's a machine around the corner."

The woman—what was her name? Some sort of flower. Lily? Yes, that was it—pulled a series of ones from the pocket of her jeans. "Okay, but no caffeine. And get one for your sister, too."

She looked at Noah then, her green eyes void of the anxiety that had been there before. "Thank you for taking them. I…hated to disappoint them."

"No worries, ma'am. I'm pretty sure they enjoyed themselves." He turned his attention to her daughter. "Right, Piper?"

"Right!"

They both chuckled at her daughter's exuberance.

He eyed the woman again. She'd tucked her long reddish-blond hair into a crude ponytail, making him wonder if she'd gotten sick again after they left. "I trust you're doing all right?"

The pink in her cheeks heightened as she tugged on the hem of her fitted gray button-down. "I am. Thank you again."

"Good." Suddenly uneasy, he glanced down the corridor. "If you'll excuse me, I have something I need to tend to."

"Of course."

With the voices of Lily and Piper echoing in his ears, he rounded the corner and headed down the corridor. Passing the alcove where the soda and snack machines were, he saw no sign of Colton.

Weird. Had Noah been so lost in thought that he'd passed him without even realizing?

Continuing on to the tack room, he spotted the boy. And his heart sank.

There, beside the bridle rack, Colton was stooped over a bucket of horseshoes. Horseshoes meant to be given to kids as souvenirs. Instead, Colton grabbed two, stuffing one into each of the pockets of his Nike hoodie.

He was stealing.

"Colton." Noah kept his voice firm, all the while keeping it void of any accusation.

The boy jerked his head up. "I…couldn't find the soda machine."

"And the horseshoes?"

Colton looked everywhere but at Noah. "I was just looking at them."

"If you want one, all you have to do is ask."

The kid's green eyes narrowed. "They're just stupid old horseshoes. Who'd want one of those?"

Noah shook his head. He'd hoped the kid would at least acknowledge his curiosity. Instead, he'd lied. And there was no way Noah could tolerate that.

He took hold of Colton's arm. "Let's go see your mother."

"Why?" The boy's voice held a note of terror as he jerked free and started down the hallway.

"I think you know why." Noah could understand the kid's attitude, but lying was a different ball game altogether.

Rounding into the lobby with Colton in tow, he saw the bewildered look in Lily's eyes as she rose from the old pew.

Grateful no one else was present, he said, "I caught this young man stealing."

"I didn't steal anything!"

Noah glared down at the boy. "Care to show me what's in your pockets?"

Colton promptly turned his pants pockets inside out to show them empty. "He's lying, Mom. I didn't take anything. See?"

A confused Lily looked from her son to Noah.

Undeterred, Noah said, "And your jacket pockets?"

The boy hesitated then. "This is stupid, Mom. I didn't take anything. You believe me, don't you?"

His mother's confused and seemingly pained gaze moved between Colton and Noah. Once. Twice.

Finally, "If there's nothing there, then you should have no problem showing us, Colton."

After a few moments, the boy pulled out the horseshoes and thrust them at Noah, the clanking of metal echoing through the small space. "They're just stupid horseshoes. You have a ton of them."

The look on Lily's face flitted between horror, disappointment and panic in a matter of seconds.

What saddened Noah the most was that he would have given the kid the horseshoes if he'd asked. But Colton hadn't asked. He'd simply taken something that didn't belong to him. Then compounded matters by lying.

Noah knew what he would do if this were his son. Question was, what would his city-slicker mother do? Offer to pay for it? Call it a misunderstanding?

That was the problem with today's world. Too many parents eager to bail their kids out instead of letting them face the consequences for their actions.

"Colton…take your sister to the car and wait for me there, please." With her arms crossed, Lily's eyes never left Noah's.

Yep, she was going to pay for her son's transgressions.

"But, Mom—"

"*Now*, Colton." She watched as the two moved slowly out the wooden door, then faced Noah. "Any chance we could work something out?"

All that was missing now was the checkbook. "Depends what you mean by 'work something out.'"

She hesitated. "I don't want my son to grow up thinking that money is the answer. He made a bad choice. He needs to learn that there are consequences for bad choices."

Her words had Noah taking a step back. He cleared his throat. "Yes, of course."

"Some parents are all too happy to pay for their kids' mistakes, but I'm not one of those people. I want Colton— and Piper—to know that every choice has a consequence. And I want them to learn now, while they're young."

Hmm… He couldn't have said it better himself. "That's commendable."

She glared at him. "I'm not looking for any commendations, Mr. Stephens. I simply want my children to grow up to be good people."

Okay, so he'd definitely underestimated her. "All right then. What if we had him work it off?"

The light in her green eyes shifted. "I like that." She hesitated then. "Depending on what you have in mind."

Ah, now he got it. Pay the consequences without really paying the consequences. "I was thinking he could come by tomorrow morning and muck out the horse stalls."

Lily choked back a laugh. Something he found rather cute. "That's perfect."

"Really?"

"Yes. Of course, it'll be 'stupid.'" She made air quotes with her long fingers.

"Of course."

Her expression softened. "But I think it'll drive home the message."

"That stealing is wrong."

"Among other things, yes."

The heel of his boot scraped across the concrete floor. "Okay, so what time can I expect him?"

"The earlier the better. How about seven?"

"In the morning?" Humph. He would have taken her for a not-before-ten kind of girl.

"You don't think I'm going to let him sleep in, do you?"

"I...obviously wasn't thinking. My apologies."

She studied him, a smile playing on her lips. "I believe in teaching my children values. So I will see you in the morning." With that, she turned and marched out the door, passing his father as she went.

Moving beside Noah, Clint Stephens watched after her. "She's pretty."

Noah made a quick left into the office. "Is she?" He grabbed the day's consent forms. "I hadn't noticed."

His father followed him. "Since when have you been blind?"

Noah chose to ignore the remark. He wasn't blind at all. But his heart belonged to his late wife, Jaycee. Now and always.

Dad paused beside the desk. "Newspaper called. Wanted to know about the ads for the rodeo school."

Noah scrubbed a hand across his face. While the new building should be completed in time for Ridgway's annual rodeo on Labor Day weekend, now that summer was here, he'd barely had any time to think about the grand opening that was supposed to coincide with the Ridgway event.

"Oh, and that Realtor called again." Dad watched him. "Have you given any more thought to renting out the cabin? Might bring you some extra income."

Noah tossed the forms into the file cabinet and threw the drawer closed with more force than he'd intended. He didn't need the extra income. He'd earned plenty during his rodeo days, made wise investments and lived modestly. Dad knew that.

And you've put all your savings into the rodeo school.

Even so, how the old man could think that he would allow strangers into the home he and his wife had once shared boggled his mind.

"Son, you know I've never been one to tell you and your brothers how to live your lives, but Jaycee's been gone twelve years now. Don't you think it's time you started living again?"

"Living?" He gestured to the stacks of papers and plans for the rodeo school. "What do you call this?"

"Oh, you're going through the motions, all right. It's just…"

"Just what?" Hands on his hips, he tried to get a handle on his annoyance.

The man looked everywhere but at Noah, then let go a sigh. "It's been a long time since you've been happy." He didn't miss the sorrow in his father's tone.

"Dad, I love this place, you know that. And the horses… I can't wait to get the rodeo school up and running."

His father held up his hands. "No need to get defensive. I believe everything you've said. I'd just hate for you to be so stuck in the past you close yourself off to the future God has in store for you."

Noah chuckled, wondering what had gotten into his father. After all, he was a widower, too. Perhaps spending so much time with his old classmate Hillary Ward-Thompson was finally getting to him. But Noah wasn't about to head down that road again. He'd loved and he'd lost. And he never wanted to feel that kind of pain ever again.

Chapter Two

Clouds dotted the sky as Lily passed under the arched metal sign that read Abundant Blessings Ranch late the next morning. She could hardly wait to hear about Colton's experience. Lord willing, three hours of mucking out stalls would teach him a lesson.

A shudder ran through her as she approached the stable, though this time it had nothing to do with equines. Hands tightening around the leather-wrapped steering wheel, she stared straight ahead. Colton was becoming so much like his father it was scary. The lies, the bullying, now stealing...

God, please help me to train my son up in the way he should go.

Something that wasn't always easy for a single parent. Especially when the other parent didn't share your faith. Not that Wade ever spent any time with his kids. Even during their visitation, they were often left in someone else's care. Because Wade didn't care about anything but himself and having a good time.

Unfortunately, it was Colton who suffered the most. Like most young boys, he wanted his father's approval. And, apparently, he thought that behaving like him was a means of getting it.

Only one of many reasons she'd wanted to get the kids away from the city. And while they usually took an extended summer trip, this year she hadn't wanted to go somewhere exotic or to some exclusive resort. That was Wade's style, not hers. She wanted something simpler. Something meaningful.

Okay, so it hadn't even been a week since they arrived in Ouray. Still, she'd never expected things could actually get worse.

By the time she and Piper stepped out of their SUV, Lily had determined that there would be no TV, handheld devices or computers of any kind for Colton for at least a week. And if he pulled another stunt, or she caught him lying, his sentence would be even longer.

That should provide the perfect opportunity for plenty more Jeep rides and family hikes. Maybe the kids would enjoy exploring some of the old mining towns that dotted the area. Anything that didn't involve horses was fine by her.

Inside the stable, she spotted her son midway down the wide corridor, standing on the bottom rung of the pipe fencing that surrounded the practice arena in the center of the building. His arms were draped over the top of the fence as he watched something or someone inside the arena. Whatever it was had certainly captured his interest, because not only had he not noticed her or his sister, he was completely engrossed. Something Lily had rarely witnessed outside of his video games.

Evidently noticing her brother, Piper let go of Lily's hand and ran ahead of her, sending dust flying from her sneakers. "Colton!"

He looked their way and, to Lily's surprise, actually smiled. He hopped down off the fence. "Mom, you wouldn't believe all the horses Noah has."

Funny, if Piper had made that same remark he would have belittled her the way he had yesterday when she pointed out the horseshoe.

"Wanna see them?"

That would be the last thing she wanted to do on such a beautiful day. Or any other day, for that matter. Still, she was happy to see him so animated.

"He's even got one that can do tricks."

"Oh." Piper's eyes widened. "I wanna see the horse that does tricks."

"And look at that, Mom." Colton pointed into the arena, where Noah was standing beside a young man on horse-back.

"What are they doing?"

Her son's gaze never left the horse. "Noah's teaching him how to rope."

"What does that mean?" Piper poked her head between the rungs for a better view.

"Just watch," said Colton.

Noah stepped away from the boy then. "Go!"

Suddenly, on the other side of the dirt-covered ring, an all-terrain vehicle sprang to life, driven by another cowboy, pulling something that looked like a small cow with horns, except with a wheel at the front. As it moved around the ring, the hind legs bobbed as though it were running.

Behind that, the horse and rider took off, the rider swinging a rope in one hand. As they approached the makeshift cow, the rider sent the rope flying.

"He did it!" Colton thrust a fist into the air as the rope fell around the horns. He looked at Lily, his smile wide. "That guy's been practicing all morning. He finally got it."

She loved teachable moments like this. "Like they say,

practice makes perfect. If you want something, you have to be willing to work for it."

He looked toward the rider, who was getting ready to go again. "He's sure been working, all right."

"And all that hard work paid off." She draped an arm around her son's shoulder. "How did things go today?"

"Good."

That was vague.

Just then, she saw Noah coming across the arena, looking all cowboy and sending a wave of unease rippling through her. She hoped Colton had done the work he was assigned. But what if he hadn't or if he had been a problem?

"Hello again," Noah said.

"Hello." Lily watched as he deftly climbed the fence, swinging one long leg over, then the other, as though he'd done it a million times before. Next thing she knew, he was beside them.

"You'll be happy to know that Colton did a real good job. Did everything I asked him to, didn't argue much."

Her son's head shot up. "I didn't argue. Did I?"

The man grinned. "No, you didn't. I just wanted to see if you were paying attention."

Colton relaxed then. "Good. 'Cause I can't wait to come back."

Lily's smile faded, her stomach muscles tightening. "Come back? You mean you want to go riding again?"

"Yeah, kinda. But what I really want is to learn to rope. With Noah."

"Oh." Uncertain how she felt about that, Lily's gaze drifted to the cowboy.

His dark eyes held an air of guilt. Had he been planting ideas in her son's head? "In addition to trail rides, we also offer riding and rodeo lessons."

She felt her own eyes widen. "Rodeo?" The last thing she wanted was to see her son bucked off some unruly bull or equine the way she had been all those years ago.

"Well, that's kind of an overarching term. Roping is only one part of rodeo. One that starts with learning how to use the rope correctly. It takes patience and discipline, but if he's persistent…"

"I'm sure I can learn."

Had she ever seen her son this enthusiastic about anything? Especially something that involved work? While she didn't relish the idea of spending so much time with a bunch of horses, patience and discipline were things Colton desperately needed to learn. Perhaps this sort of training—any training—could be good for him. Give him something to focus on besides himself.

Tucking her fear aside, Lily addressed Noah. "How much do the lessons cost?"

He tipped his cowboy hat back with a smile. "They won't cost you a thing."

She bristled. "Nothing is ever free, Mr. Stephens." In her experience, people always expected something.

"I said it wouldn't cost *you* anything."

She eyed him curiously, waiting for him to explain.

"Colton tells me you're in Ouray for the summer."

"That's correct."

"Well, he's the one who wants lessons." He turned his attention to her son. "And we could use another hand around here. What if we worked out a trade? You muck out the stalls three days a week in exchange for three days of lessons."

The elation on her son's face only added to her dilemma. "Can I, Mom? Please?"

She studied the rafters overhead, uncertain how to respond. If she said no, she'd be the bad guy. But while she liked the idea of Colton working and appreciated his excitement, she was still skeptical. And not only about the horses.

Her gaze shifted to Noah. Why was this long, tall cowboy being so nice after Colton stole from him? Was he simply trying to get some free labor or did he genuinely want to help her son?

No matter which way she looked at it, she couldn't help wondering what this arrangement might cost her in the long run.

"That's good, Colton, but you need to twist your wrist like this." Standing alongside the boy in the arena the next morning, Noah demonstrated. "Which also turns the rope so it will lie properly as you're coiling it."

"Like this?" The boy ran a gloved hand down the length he held, then twisted his wrist outward the way Noah had.

"Now you're getting it." Noah's gaze inadvertently veered toward the aluminum bleachers outside the arena where Lily and Piper had been throughout Colton's lesson. Why had Lily been so cynical when he offered to teach Colton in exchange for some work? As if he was trying to take advantage of them. Wasn't his word good enough?

The kid looked up at him. "It feels kinda weird."

He again gave the boy his full attention. Or at least tried to. He sure hoped Colton's mother wasn't planning to be there for all of his lessons. Given her fear of horses, though, Noah had a feeling she'd be front and center for each and every one.

"At first, yes. But as you practice, it'll become second nature."

Colton tossed out his rope again, and a few moments

later, he had it perfectly coiled. "Look, I did it." He held it up. "It looks just like yours."

His enthusiasm warmed Noah's heart. This was what he loved about teaching kids. Sharing in their sense of accomplishment.

"Remember what I said yesterday about practice, patience and persistence?"

"Yeah."

Noah lifted a brow, careful not to look too stern. "How about we say 'yes, sir'?"

A hint of pink crept into the kid's cheeks. "Yes, sir."

Noah smiled then. "You exercised both patience and persistence as you practiced coiling that rope until you finally got it right."

The kid was quiet for a moment. "Can I keep practicing?"

"Not only can you, you have to." Noah tossed his rope out. "The more you practice—" he began to reel it in "—the more used to it you become." He held up his freshly coiled rope.

"Awesome." Colton practically beamed as he made another attempt.

Noah, however, found his thoughts preoccupied once again by the boy's mother. Why did it chafe him so that Lily had questioned his integrity?

He glanced from Colton to Lily to one of the hands who was tending to the horses. Because in his world, integrity was everything. A man without honor was nothing but a coward in his book. And for some strange reason, he wanted Lily and her children to see him as honorable.

He shook his head. Ridiculous. Why should he care what they thought? They were strangers. Which made his reaction even more preposterous.

"How come I'm not on a horse?"

He jerked his gaze back to Colton, annoyed that he'd allowed himself to be distracted. "There are two parts to roping. Rope handling and horsemanship. You have to learn both, though we won't put the two together for a while yet. We'll work with a horse during your next lesson."

"Next lesson? You mean we're done already?"

"We've been working for almost two hours." And Lily had been watching them from the second row the entire time.

Colton's eyes widened. "Really?"

"Time flies when you're having fun."

"Yea— Yes, sir."

Noah ruffled the kid's sandy brown hair. "Good boy."

Out of the corner of his eye, he saw his father take a seat beside Lily.

She smiled as they talked, making Noah uneasy. What were they discussing? Colton? The weather? After Dad's little talk the other day, not to mention his comment about Lily being pretty, there was no telling what the old man was apt to say.

Noah cringed at the possibilities.

"Okay, Colton, how about we plan to meet again Monday morning?"

"Aww, but I'm just getting good."

"All right then, you can keep practicing while I go talk to your mother." Because the more he saw Lily laugh, the more he wanted to know what she and his father were discussing.

A few minutes later, he hopped the fence to join the three of them. "What's going on?"

Hands clasped, forearms on his thighs, his father looked up at him. "Lily here was just telling me that she plans a lot of charity events back in Denver."

"That's nice." He glanced at Lily. Dressed in jeans and riding boots with a navy blazer over a white T-shirt, she looked ready for English riding. Something she wasn't likely to find at Abundant Blessings Ranch.

"*Big* events." Dad's dark brown eyes glinted with pleasure. "Like *grand openings*."

Noah glared at his father, knowing good and well what he was up to. He wanted Lily to help them. Well, Noah wasn't biting.

"Mommy gave me the best princess birthday party ever." Piper moved behind her mother, snaking her arms around Lily's shoulders.

"I see." Birthday parties. Kids' parties, at that. Not exactly the kind of event he had in mind.

"She also hosted Denver's Oil Baron's Ball," said Dad.

Noah lifted his hat to scratch his head. Okay, so that was a little higher up the scale. Still, that didn't mean Lily should help him.

Straightening, his father twisted to give Lily his full attention. "Did you know that Noah is in the process of expanding our little riding school?"

She peered up at Noah. "I heard mention of rodeo lessons."

Noah cleared his throat. "Actually, we're expanding to a year-round rodeo school." He shifted from one foot to the next. "The new arena is still under construction, but it should be ready sometime in August."

"Is that the building going up next door?" She pointed in the general vicinity.

"Sure is," Dad answered before Noah even had a chance. "The grand opening is set for Labor Day weekend to coincide with the annual rodeo in Ridgway. Problem is that Noah doesn't have any time to promote or plan the event." He shrugged. "Not that he really knows much about that sort of thing."

Noah shook his head. He knew the old man was trying to help, that he wanted the rodeo school to succeed every bit as much as Noah did, but sometimes he just didn't know when to shut up.

"Dad, I—"

"Mom could help you. She knows all about planning stuff."

Noah jerked his head to discover Colton standing beside him. "I thought you were practicing."

The boy lowered his gaze. "It wasn't as fun without you."

Noah's heart swelled, though he quickly tamped it down. "Your mom is on vacation, Colton."

"I know, but she always says parties and stuff aren't really work." He looked at Lily. "Right, Mom?"

The poor woman seemed to be at a loss for words. She was no more interested in giving Noah her help than he was in receiving it. Yet while he'd come to accept that he did, indeed, need some sort of help, he'd prefer to hire someone local. Someone familiar with rodeo. Not a city girl who was afraid of horses.

He set a hand on Colton's shoulder. "Colton, that's not fair to your mom. You all are here because she wants to spend time with you and Piper, not some grungy old cowboys."

"That's okay," chimed Piper. "We can help, too."

"Yeah," said Colton. "We'll still be together."

Dad stood then. "I'm afraid Noah's right, kids. It's not fair to volunteer your mother like that."

Noah's brow lifted. Dad was the one who started this whole discussion.

"Thank you for understanding." Lily reached for Colton's hand. "This summer is all about my kids."

"As it should be." Ignoring the unexpected wave of disappointment that came over him, he studied the woman laughing with her children. Lily might know how to put on a good party, but she was the wrong candidate for this job.

Chapter Three

Lily stood at the top of Hurricane Pass the next afternoon, savoring the breathtaking view. At more than twelve thousand feet, it felt as though she was on top of the world.

Brown, barren peaks stretched out before her as far as she could see, while lush green mingled with patches of snow across their rocky slopes. She drew in a long breath of crisp mountain air. Simply glorious.

This was exactly what she'd envisioned when she decided to bring the kids to Ouray. Jeep rides in the mountains, exploring God's creation…togetherness.

"What do you guys think?" She eyed her children, who had finally stopped throwing snowballs at each other long enough to join her.

"Spectacular!" Her daughter tossed her arms wide in typical Piper fashion.

"It's okay." Hands shoved in the pockets of his hoodie, Colton squinted against the sun. "It would be cooler on a horse."

Lily tried to keep her groan to herself. She was beginning to regret ever having taken the kids to Abundant Blessings Ranch. All she'd heard about the past four days was horses, riding, roping... Not to mention how she should help Noah with the rodeo school's grand opening.

Her gaze drifted to the glacial blue waters of Lake Como just below where she stood. She was not here to plan an event. Especially the grand opening of a rodeo school. Spending this summer as a family, teaching her children to enjoy the simple things in life was what was important to her.

What could be simpler than spending time on a real ranch with good, hardworking people and beautiful animals?

Horses might be beautiful, but she still didn't want to be around them. Or their cowboy owner.

You could at least consider helping Noah.

The thought stiffened her spine. And allow herself to be taken advantage of, the way she had when she was with Wade Davis? No, thank you.

When they returned to town a few hours later, Lily walked along Main Street with her children, allowing them to peruse a couple of souvenir shops while she relished the remarkable view. Unlike most towns where the mountains sat in the distance, Ouray was literally enveloped by them. No matter which way she looked, the mountains were right there. Only part of what made this town so appealing. Throw in the gorgeous Victorian-era buildings, friendly people and colorful baskets of flowers hanging from every lamppost, and she was smitten.

"Afternoon, Lily."

She turned to see Clint Stephens. "Hello, Mr. Stephens."

Hands dangling from the pockets of his Wrangler jeans, he glanced around. "Where are Colton and Piper?"

"In the gift sho—" She spotted the pair exiting the store. "Make that right here."

"Hi, Mr. Stephens." Their collective greeting revealed how genuinely happy they were to see him.

"What have you kids been up to today? Did you do anything fun?"

"We went to the top of the world," said Piper.

"Top of world?" Clint eyed Lily as a motorcycle rumbled past.

"We took a Jeep tour up to Hurricane Pass."

"Oh." He looked at Piper again. "Then I guess you were way up there."

"I'm hungry." Colton moved beside Lily. "What's for dinner?"

She was surprised he'd gone this long without asking. Save for a small snack, he hadn't eaten since lunch.

"Honestly, I haven't given it much thought, but I'm sure we can find something at the house."

"I'm on my way over to Granny's Kitchen to grab some dinner." Clint looked at each of them. "Would you three care to join me?"

Piper gasped while her brother's eyes and smile grew wide.

"Could we?" said Colton. "We haven't eaten there yet."

Beside him, Piper prayed her hands together. "Please…"

Lily noted the sun hovering over the town's western slope. "I guess it has been a while since we've gone out to eat." Besides, she really wasn't up to fixing a meal tonight. "Are you sure you don't mind, Mr. Stephens?"

"Course not. It'll save me from eating alone."

"Okay then."

Inside the quaint restaurant situated on a corner farther down the street, the four of them sat down in a booth by the window, allowing them to enjoy the view.

"Granny's Kitchen is as close to home cooking as you're going to get." Clint removed his cowboy hat and slid in beside Colton. "And everything on the menu is good." He ran a callused hand through his thick salt-and-pepper hair.

A waitress approached. Blonde, closer to Clint's age and very well put together, from her perfectly styled short hair to her chic red patent leather ballet flats. "Looks like you've got some company, Clint." She set four waters on the high-gloss wooden table top, then handed menus to each of them, along with crayons for the kids, before laying a hand on Clint's shoulder.

"Hillary, this is Lily—" he gestured "—and her children, Colton and Piper."

Lily held out her hand. "It's nice to meet you, Hillary."

The woman took hold, her grip firm. "Are you in town on vacation?"

"For the summer, yes."

"Well, we're glad to have you." Hillary eyed each of them. "I'll give you minute to look over those menus." With that she was gone.

Noting the familiarity between the two, Lily watched the older man. "Is that your wife?"

"Hillary?" Clint blushed. "No, she's just an old friend. My wife died three years ago."

"I'm sorry to hear that."

"I won't try to kid you, it was rough. But God has a plan."

"Yes, He does." Reaching for her water, she eyed the waitress behind the counter. Either Clint was unaware of Hillary's feelings toward him or simply refused to acknowledge them. Whatever the case, Lily suspected they were more than just friends.

After turning in their orders, Lily rested her forearms on the edge of the table, curiosity niggling at her brain.

After all, with Colton taking lessons, she owed it to herself to learn as much about his instructor as she could.

"Tell me about this rodeo school Noah plans to open."

The man smiled like any proud father. "Noah's always had a gift for teaching and a heart for kids." He unwrapped his silverware and set the napkin in his lap. "This school has been his dream ever since he left the rodeo circuit."

"He was a bull rider?" Lily regretted the surprise in her voice.

Clint's amused grin was worth it, though. "Yes, but horses were always his specialty. He gets that from his mama."

"Why was the rodeo school Noah's dream?" Colton watched the older man intently.

"He...went through some hard times." Fingering the unopened straw atop the table, he continued, "The rodeo—horses, in particular—helped him get back in the saddle, so to speak."

Hard times? That could be almost anything. Drugs. Alcohol. But she wasn't about to pry.

"What kind of hard times?"

"Colton!" Lily cringed.

"It's all right." The corners of Clint's mouth tipped upward once again. "Can't blame the boy for being curious." He looked at Colton. "Noah lost some people that were very special to him."

"Like his mommy?" Crayon still in hand, Piper looked up from her colorful place mat.

"That's right." Clint turned his attention to Lily. "Rodeo helped him cope."

She watched the man across from her. "Was he any good?"

Clint's grin seemed laced with as much sorrow as

pride. "When you have nothing to lose, you tend to put it all out there."

Nothing to lose? What did that mean?

Curious, Lily wanted to know more. So after the kids went to bed that night, she searched the internet for Noah Stephens and came up with a plethora of articles, photos and videos.

She clicked on the first link.

After the deaths of his wife and unborn child...

Lily found herself blinking back emotion. Though her ex-husband was still very much alive, she understood how it felt to lose someone you love. But to lose a child, too... She couldn't imagine how painful that must have been.

She clicked on another link. *The man had no fear. Every time he went out there, it was as though he was challenging God to take him, too.*

When you have nothing to lose, you tend to put it all out there, Clint had said. *Rodeo helped him.*

She swiped at a wayward tear that trailed down her cheek. No wonder the rodeo school was so important to Noah. And he did seem to be good with the kids. In fact, Colton had rarely responded so well to a stranger.

Still...

She drew in a breath. That didn't mean *she* had to help him.

Monday was a busy one for Noah. Aside from lessons and numerous people wanting trail rides, he still needed to run into town to drop off his ad for the July Fourth edition of the newspaper. Next week, thousands of people would flood Ouray for its annual Fourth of July celebration, which was as unique as the town itself. Giving Noah the perfect opportunity to let everyone know about the rodeo school. Some of those visitors might even be persuaded to return in September for the school's grand opening and Ridgway's Labor Day rodeo.

But first he needed to concentrate on helping Colton with his riding lesson.

Boots firmly in the dirt, he watched as Colton made a practice run around the arena. He was surprised by how quickly the boy was catching on. The fact that he had a positive attitude was a big help. It seemed that whenever Colton showed up, whether to work or learn, he was ready to give it his all. A far cry from the cantankerous, smart-mouthed kid Noah had met last week. Sure, there'd been a few complaints, but overall, the kid was as eager to help as he was to learn. Like he'd found his calling. Or just someplace to direct his pent-up anger.

And Noah was more than happy to help.

He took hold of the quarter horse's bridle as the kid approached. "Good job, Colton."

"That was fun." The boy leaned forward to stroke the animal's mane.

Sonic nickered in response.

"You hear that? I think Sonic likes you."

"He's a good horse."

"Yes, he is." Not to mention experienced, which was why Noah had chosen him. "Now, when you're roping and riding, you're going to need your hands to control the rope."

The kid cocked his head, his brow marked with confusion. "So how do you hold on to the reins?"

"You don't." Noah couldn't help grinning. "Let me show you something." He moved beside the horse. "Let go of the reins."

Colton complied.

"Now pull your legs together so they're pressing into Sonic's sides."

"Like this?"

Noah knew the boy was doing it correctly when Sonic dropped his head and began to back up.

The kid's eyes widened. "Did I make him do that?"

"You sure did."

"That is so cool." His excitement echoed from the rafters.

"When roping, a rider has to know how to control the horse without using his hands. We'll work on that more next time."

"Aw, we're done already?" He reached for the reins, slapping them against his leg.

"Afraid so. I've got something I need to take care of in town."

"Okay…" The boy reluctantly dismounted, the leather of the saddle creaking.

"Why don't you take ol' Sonic here back to his stall while I talk to your mom?"

"Can I give him some horse cookies?"

"A couple, yes."

While Colton headed off with the horse, Noah made his way to the opposite side of the arena to talk with Lily. She was sitting alone in her usual spot on the bleachers.

"The kid's a natural." He hopped the fence.

"Really?" Lily stood, her long hair spilling over her shoulders. "He must get it from his grandmother then, because it certainly didn't come from me."

"Mommy?" An excited Piper skipped toward them, her ponytail bobbing, while Noah's father followed a short distance behind.

"What is it, Piper?" Lily laid a hand on her daughter's back as if to settle her.

"Mr. Stephens said I can have a soda if it's all right with you. Can I?"

"Piper's been working hard, helping me clean the riding helmets." Dad grinned at the child. "Would it be all right if I rewarded her with a soda?"

"Of course." Lily looked at her daughter. "But nothing caffeinated."

"Okay." Piper took hold of his father's hand.

Noah couldn't help smiling. She was a cutie with a personality to match. And just like his nieces, she brought out the best in his old man.

"Newspaper called." Dad's voice pulled him from his thoughts.

He looked at his father.

"They said you missed the deadline for advertising in the July Fourth edition."

"No, I didn't." He shook his head. "The cutoff is tomorrow. I'm planning to drop the ad by the newspaper office in just a little bit."

"The deadline was noon today."

"Noon?" He looked at his watch. It was almost three. Then he remembered that they'd moved the deadline up a day this week due to the holiday. His stomach clenched. How could he have forgotten something so important? His life savings were riding on the success of the rodeo school.

He glanced in Lily's direction to discover her watching him.

Just what he needed. Why'd his father have to bring that up in front of her?

"Mom, did you see me out there?" Colton approached, his smile wide.

"Yes. You looked very handsome."

"Mr. Stephens said I could have a soda." Piper peered up at her brother. "Maybe he'll let you have one, too."

"Can I?" Colton looked to the older man.

"Sure. Come on, you two."

As the trio headed down the corridor, Noah sensed Lily was still watching him. But he didn't dare turn around.

"You know—" he heard her boots against the bleachers before she stepped in front of him "—an interview with the newspaper might garner more attention than an ad. Besides, you have to pay for advertising. Interviews are free."

He stared down at her, still frustrated. "What would they interview me about?"

Her expression went flat. "You're a former rodeo champion who's opening a rodeo school. And not just any rodeo champ, but one of the best champions ever."

He studied her, his gaze narrowing. "How do you know that?"

She shrugged. "The internet."

She'd googled him? Why? "Don't believe everything you read." He turned, ready to leave.

"Well, unless somebody made up those stats…"

He paused then and faced her again. "Do you really see me going to the newspaper and asking them to interview me?"

"No." She crossed her arms over her chest. "First you have to create interest. Say, in the form of a press release." She was talking way over his head.

He set his hands on his hips. "Lily, I don't even know what that is."

"Maybe not—" she inched toward him "—but I do."

He wasn't in the mood for games. "What is that supposed to mean?"

"It means—" with only a short distance between them, she dropped her arms to her sides "—that I'm willing to help you promote the rodeo school and get ready for its grand opening."

"Why would you do that?"

Seemingly frustrated, she gestured around the arena. "My kids are completely enamored with this place. And you." Her sideways glance hinted at annoyance. "Meaning we'll likely be spending a lot of time here this summer. Especially now that Piper wants to take lessons. So I may as well make myself useful."

A woman who was scared to death of horses wanted to help him promote the rodeo school? That had to be one of the craziest things he'd ever heard.

She was right about one thing, though. With both of her kids becoming more and more entrenched in events at the ranch, she'd likely be here a lot. At least helping with the rodeo school would give her something to do besides hover during the kids' lessons.

He contemplated her a moment. What if she did help him? In the last two minutes alone, he'd seen that she knew way more about publicizing something than he did. Still, her fear of horses gave him pause.

"Perhaps I could give you riding lessons, too. I mean, if you're helping me with the promotion."

She straightened, her shoulders rigid, her expression pinched. "That's highly doubtful, Mr. Stephens."

Her quick response almost made him laugh. Because there was nothing he enjoyed more than a good challenge. And getting Lily comfortable around horses was a huge one.

Of course, he also knew when to loosen the reins. "Okay, then I will take you up on your offer, on one condition."

One perfectly arched brow lifted in question.

"That you call me Noah. Mr. Stephens is my dad."

Chapter Four

Lily aimed her SUV north on Highway 550 just before noon the next day. Passing the Ouray city limits sign, she tried to figure out what had compelled her to take on the role of promoter for the rodeo school. She'd even gone so far as to talk Noah into it. And, in the process, she'd taken a giant step out of her element. What did she know about rodeo? What about the panic that threatened to set in whenever she was around horses?

She eyed the rushing waters of the Uncompahgre River to her left. Perhaps it was the pride in Clint's eyes when he talked about Noah's dream that had persuaded her. Or maybe it was the tough-but-tender manner Noah had with Colton. Encouraging him and gently correcting, instead of belittling him the way Colton's father so often did.

Her grip firm on the steering wheel, she maneuvered her vehicle past the red sandstone walls to her right. She'd seen the sadness in Noah's dark eyes on more than one occasion. Yet it couldn't have been the sudden knowledge of what he'd gone through that had spurred her.

No, she simply needed something to keep herself occupied while the kids were busy at the ranch.

"Mommy, when am I going to start *my* riding lessons?" In the rearview mirror, she noticed Piper watching her.

"I'm not sure, honey. Noah had to check his schedule." A schedule that seemed to be getting fuller all the time, making Lily wonder when she'd be able to sit him down for a little Q and A. Because whether she wanted to or not, she was going to have to learn more about this rodeo school. Something that inevitably meant spending way more time with Noah and those horses than she cared to. However, if she was going to tackle this job to the best of her ability, she had no other choice. Her reputation was at stake.

That's it!

Smiling, she bumped her vehicle over the cattle guard at Abundant Blessings Ranch. She'd simply think of this job as a challenge. Something that would stretch her and help hone her skills. After all, she'd already been thinking about turning her enjoyment of event planning into a business. This would be one event she could add to her résumé that would be different from anything else she'd ever done. However, she prayed she'd never have to do anything with horses ever again.

Excitement filled her as they pulled up to the stable. If she could bring about a successful launch for the rodeo school, she should be able to tackle anything.

Under a cloudless sky, she shifted her SUV into Park, turned off the ignition and exited, noting the numerous other vehicles parked in the area, even overflowing the small gravel parking lot onto the grass. Why were they so busy?

She released a frustrated sigh. Busy didn't bode well for her plans of a meeting with Noah.

Inside the stable's rustic lobby, at least a dozen people stood waiting while Noah passed out paperwork and pens.

He spotted her. "Colton's practicing in the arena." He nodded in that direction before disappearing into the office.

She followed him. Watched as he added paperwork to two more clipboards. "I have several questions I need to ask you about the rodeo school."

"Such as?" He grabbed a handful of pens from a small basket.

"For starters, I'd like more information about your rodeo days so I can start getting some interviews set up. I could take the kids to get some lunch and come back. Perhaps things will have slowed down."

"Sorry, Lily, but between lessons and fully booked trail rides, I'm busier than a termite in a sawmill." He nudged the brim of his cowboy hat, tilting it up ever so slightly as his eyes met hers. "Any chance you could come back this evening? Say around six?"

"Oh." Disappointment had her gaze falling to the concrete floor. "Sure, I can do that." Lifting her head, she sent him her best smile. "I need to do some more research on media outlets, anyway."

He grinned then. "Great. I'll see you this evening."

While Lily had every intention of doing that research, those notions came to a screeching halt once she and her children returned to town. Suddenly, Colton was the one ready to do some exploring. It was an opportunity she wasn't about to pass up. So, after a quick round of sandwiches at the mountainside cabin she'd rented for the summer, the three of them went to Box Canyon, where they hiked deep into the gorge to see a powerful waterfall, then climbed up the hillside to the high bridge that not only spanned the gorge but offered the most incredible view of the town she was quickly growing to love.

By the time she was finally able to drag Piper away from all the chipmunks that called the area around Box

Canyon home, it was almost four o'clock, leaving them just enough time to grab an ice-cream cone and enjoy the views on Main Street before heading back to the ranch.

Clint was there to greet them when they pulled up to the stable at six o'clock, and she couldn't help wondering if he was there to run interference for a still-busy Noah. He waited beside the front door as they got out of the SUV.

"I wasn't expecting to see you all this late in the day." He tipped his hat in greeting.

Shielding her eyes from the sun, Lily tucked the electronic tablet she used to take notes under her arm. "I'm here to meet with Noah."

"Well." The older man chuckled. "I was just coming to get him. We're having a family cookout up at the house tonight."

Noah hadn't said anything about a cookout. Then again, he had been pretty busy when she stopped by earlier.

"Why don't you and the kids join us for supper?"

While her children's eyes went wide, Lily hesitated. "We don't want to interrupt a family meal."

"Nonsense." Clint waved off her objection. "We just call it a family supper, but that doesn't mean other people can't come. There's always plenty of food." His gaze moved between the children. "Besides, my granddaughters are here, and they'd enjoy having someone else their age."

"How old are they?" Colton appeared as curious as he was apprehensive.

Clint rubbed his chin. "Let's see. I believe Megan is eleven now—she's turning into quite the horsewoman— and Kenzie's five."

Right about her kids' ages. And while it would be nice, they hadn't come for dinner.

"Can we, Mom?" Colton's interest had definitely been piqued. "We haven't had dinner yet."

"No, but we're here so I can meet with Noah."

Just then, the wooden front door creaked open, and the cowboy exited the stable. "I thought I heard voices out here."

"I was just telling Lily and kids they should join us for our cookout," said Clint.

Noah eyes seemed to narrow. "What cookout?"

"Son, you know we always have family dinners."

"Yes, sir, but they're usually on Sundays."

"Or any other time that suits us." Clint scowled. "Especially when the weather is as nice as it is today. So, if you all would care to join me back at the house…" With that, he started up the gravel drive.

Colton and Piper sent her pleading gazes.

"Go ahead." Lily watched the two kids rush after the older man. They were growing more fond of him by the day.

"We'd better join them, you know," said Noah.

She reached for her tablet and clutched it in both hands. "What about our meeting? Unless you think we could talk over dinner." Far away from all those horses. That would be the best of both worlds. She'd get the information she needed and a good meal, too.

Noah shrugged. "We could try, but with the whole family here, an in-depth conversation isn't likely."

"I see."

"Of course, we could always slip back inside the stable and talk. The kids would be occupied—"

"No way." She held up a hand. "I'm not going to be responsible for keeping you from a family meal." *Nice cover.*

"All right then." He eyed the single-story house that sat farther up the drive. "I guess we'd better join them."

She thumped the tablet against her leg, still torn. "Let me put this in the car."

Though it wasn't a long walk, she decided to seize the

only opportunity she'd had all day. "What drew you to rodeo?"

He stared out over the green, cattle-dotted pasture as gravel crunched beneath their steps. "I suppose it was a combination of things. To a boy growing up on a ranch, it looked like the coolest job ever. So I started honing my roping skills. Calves at first, then I worked my way up to steers. Mama taught me everything she knew about horses. Next thing I knew I was bronc riding, then bull riding—"

A gentle breeze had her hair brushing against her cheek.

She tucked it behind her ear. "Weren't you afraid?"

He lifted a shoulder. "At first, I suppose. But once I got good at things, I wanted to be even better."

"'Bout time you made it, bro." A tall, dark-haired man who looked very much like both Noah and his father stepped off the expansive wooden deck as they approached the cedar home. "We're getting hungry."

The corner of Noah's mouth lifted. "Lily, this is Andrew. The *annoying* brother."

"Hey…" Andrew smiled her way. "It's nice to meet you, Lily."

"Good to meet you."

"You must be Colton and Piper's mom?" A woman with blond curls and a definite baby bump approached and reached out her hand. "I'm Megan's mom, Carly Stephens."

Lily briefly took hold.

"And my wife," Andrew was quick to add, his pride as evident as it was heartwarming. Every woman should be so blessed.

"When are you due?"

The woman smoothed a hand over her flowing shirt. "September 17, give or take. You know how that goes."

She recalled her son's past-due arrival and Piper's earlier-than-expected appearance. "I certainly do."

Colton came toward her then with a cute strawberry blonde girl she guessed to be Megan. "Mom, can I go to the stable with Megan? She wants to show me her horse."

Lily shared a glance with Carly. Saw the stealthy head shake that would have gone unrecognized by anyone except another mother. "Has Megan checked with her mom?"

The grinning girl stepped toward Carly. "Can we?"

"Can you what?" Clint joined them then with the blonde from the restaurant at his side.

Lily smiled her way. "Hello, Hillary. Good to see you again."

"Are you overwhelmed yet, Lily?"

Noting about a half a dozen people still unknown to her, she had to admit— "A little, yes." And while she would have welcomed this type of event any other time, tonight it only meant that the meeting she needed to have with Noah wasn't going to happen. Her questions would go unanswered. And if Noah continued to be as busy as he was today, she might never get the information she needed.

Noah usually enjoyed family dinners. But this one was different. Because according to his brothers, the invitation had only gone out today, *after* Noah offhandedly mentioned to his father that Lily would be coming by tonight.

He eyed the old cowboy sitting on the opposite side of the wooden picnic table. It seemed ever since Andrew and Matt both got married last year, his father had grown increasingly eager to marry off the rest of his sons. And for whatever reason, he seemed to have his sights set on Noah.

But as far as he was concerned, his father was wasting his time. Noah already had a wife. And even though Jaycee had left this world, he'd vowed to love her forever, and that's exactly what he intended to do.

His gaze inadvertently drifted to Lily sitting beside him. With her reddish-blond hair and sparkling green eyes, she was, indeed, pretty. Just not Noah's type. Even if he were in the market for a wife, Lily was too much of a city girl for his tastes. Not to mention her less-than-enthusiastic feelings about horses and that she was only in Ouray for the summer.

However, she had agreed to help promote the rodeo school. Something he knew nothing about, so it was in his best interest to tell her whatever it was she was so eager to know in order to get the school off on the right foot.

He stuffed the last bite of his hamburger into his mouth and dusted off his hands. It shouldn't be that bad. After all, the rodeo school was something he could get excited about. Without rodeo, he didn't know where he'd be. And while he might have headed back into the arena with a death wish, God had used it to show him that He still had a purpose for Noah. And Noah intended to follow that calling. This world was filled with hurting people. If he could help even one of them…

"Mom," Colton came up behind them. "Me and Megan are done eating and her mom says it's okay for us to go to the stable, if it's okay with you. Can we?"

Lily pushed aside her paper plate, which was littered with celery pieces she'd picked out of her potato salad, and dabbed her mouth with a paper napkin. "Yes, you may. But I want you to be on your best behavior. I know you're familiar with the stable, but Megan has been here a lot longer than you have." She smiled up at Noah's niece, who stood beside Colton. "You do what she says. Okay?"

"I will," said the boy, and the two kids were off like a shot.

Lily peered up at Noah then. "I assume you're all right with them going."

"Yes. But, if you have reservations, we could always join them."

"Oh, that's not—"

"Maybe we could finally have that discussion about the rodeo school."

She hesitated a moment. "Or we could find a quiet place around here. I mean, what about Piper?"

"She can go with us." Turning, he eyed the ponytailed blonde giggling with Matt's daughter, Kenzie. "However, she looks like she's having a pretty good time here." He faced Lily again. "Besides, I think a tour of the stable is in order."

"Why?" She looked almost appalled. "What does a tour of the stable have to do with rodeo?"

He puffed out a laugh. "For starters, it's where I spend most of my time. It's where we train students, at least until the other building is complete."

Her deep breath gave him the feeling she was trying to talk herself into it.

"Okay. Let me check with Piper." Standing, she moved to the other table and smoothed a hand across her daughter's back.

The girl looked up at her mother.

"Noah and I are going to the stable. Would you like to go with us?"

The little girl frowned. "But Kenzie's dad said they're going to have s'mores."

Noah looked to the other side of the table, to Matt and

his wife, Lacie. "Would you two mind keeping an eye on Piper while Lily and I run down to the stable?"

"Not at all." Standing, Lacie reached for the kids' plates. "The two of them are having a good time."

"We won't be long." Lily waved to Piper, then turned and ran into another of Noah's siblings. "Oh!"

Noah caught her elbow. "Lily, this is Jude."

Her eyes went wide. "Just how many brothers do you have?"

"I'm the fourth of five Stephens' sons," offered Jude. "And it's nice to meet you."

Lily looked from Noah to Jude, who also had their father's dark hair and eyes. "Did they just clone you guys? Because all of you kind of look the same."

Jude laughed. "Not all of us." He eyed Noah. "She hasn't met Daniel yet, has she?"

Just then, the brother in question slapped him on the back. "Did I hear my name?"

"Lily," Jude started. "This is Daniel, the baby of the family."

She simply stared at the only blond, blue-eyed brother. "I guess that debunks my cloning theory. How did you—"

"Break the mold?" Daniel shrugged. "The world couldn't have handled it if they'd all been as good-looking as me."

"Oh, brother." Jude rolled his eyes. "Don't let him con you, Lily. Daniel just ended up with all of our mother's genes because Dad's finally ran out."

Noah checked his watch. At this rate, they'd never make it to the stable. "Gentlemen, you're going to have to excuse us. Lily and I have work to do."

She smiled at his brothers. "It's been a pleasure."

Twilight settled around them as they descended the steps, the air still as they started toward the stable.

"Four brothers." Lily shook her head. "I can't imagine."

"Why?" Hands in his pockets, Noah glanced up to a rising moon. "Don't you have any siblings?"

"No. I'm an only child."

"Really?" Gravel ground beneath his boots. "Now there's something I can't imagine."

She chuckled. A sweet sound he found himself longing to hear again. "Then I guess there's one thing we have in common."

Lily retrieved her tablet before heading inside with Noah.

He breathed in the comforting aromas of horse and hay. Here, he was at home.

"We built this structure a few years ago so we could offer riding lessons year-round." He moved past the lobby, toward the training arena.

Opening the cover on her tablet, Lily followed him on the same path she'd taken almost daily to observe Colton's lessons. "Why can't you use this arena for the rodeo school?"

"Too small." Turning to face her, he perched an elbow atop a fence rung. "The two buildings will be attached by a walkway, though, since the horses will still be stabled here."

She made a few notes before looking at him again. "Who designed the new arena?"

"I did. At least the general layout."

"I'm impressed." Her fingers moved over the screen once more.

"Don't be. I've been in a lot of arenas over the years. Everything from small to large, indoor and out. I know what works, and I know what we need."

She cocked her head. "Sounds like you're an expert."

He lifted a shoulder. "Perhaps the only thing I'm an expert at."

"Besides rodeo itself."

"It's what I know." He turned. "Follow me." He aimed for one of two wide corridors lined with stalls.

As they rounded the corner, Lily stopped. "Where are we going?"

"I thought I'd show you a few of the horses."

"That's...not necessary." She fidgeted with her necklace. "Really, I—I don't need to see them."

He moved closer. "I'm not talking about riding them, Lily." He studied her. Saw the flicker of fear in her eyes. "I promise, you'll be fine. I'll be right with you."

After a long moment, she nodded and started walking again.

Hoping to put her at ease, he said, "Why don't you ask me some of those questions you said you had."

"Um, okay. Uh, what drew you to the rodeo?"

He looked at her. Saw her cast a wary eye at each and every horse they passed. "You asked me that earlier. When we were walking to the house."

"I did?" She met his gaze. "Yes, that's right."

He stopped her then. "Do you always get this nervous around horses?"

Her head bobbed. "Chalk it up to a bad experience when I was a kid."

"What happened?"

Her gaze searched his, and he saw her anxiety ease for a moment.

Hugging the tablet against her chest, she said, "My mother loved horses and used to dream of me becoming a championship English rider. So, when I was four, she bought me a horse." Lily looked away then. "I can still see him staring down at me with those ominous dark eyes. Right before he bit me."

"He bit you?"

"He did. Then while I was still crying, my mother hoisted me into the saddle. Of course, the horse wasn't having any of that and promptly bucked me off, leaving me with a broken arm and a strong determination never to get on a horse again."

Noah could hardly believe what he was hearing. No parent should force their child to do something they were afraid of. Coaxing was one thing, but to put her in the saddle while she was still crying…

Briefly lifting his hat, he raked a hand through his hair. "No wonder you made yourself sick at the thought of riding."

Lily rolled her eyes. "Please, don't remind me."

"I have to say, I commend you for not placing your fears on your children. And just so you know, your mother was wrong to put you on that horse. These animals—" he motioned to the stalls on either side of them "—are very good at sensing things, including fear."

"Guess it's a good thing I didn't ride with you then." Her laugh was a nervous one. "You must think I'm a complete idiot."

"Absolutely not." Arms crossed, he rocked back on his heels. "Though I do believe I could help you overcome your fear."

"Ha! I highly doubt that."

His brow shot up. "Is that a dare?"

"More like extreme skepticism."

Lowering his arms, he looked into her green eyes, knowing he shouldn't care. What should it matter to him if she was afraid of horses? After this summer, she'd likely never be around them again.

Unfortunately, he did care.

"That's too bad. Because I've never been one to back down from a challenge." Just then, he spotted Colton and

Megan coming down the aisle. "You know, both of your kids seem quite enthralled with horses. Wouldn't it be nice if you could ride with them?"

"What are you guys doing here?" Colton asked as he approached.

"Just going over some stuff about the rodeo school." While Lily appeared calm and collected, the way she looked at her son, as though seeing him through different eyes, had Noah wondering if he'd gotten through to her. Did she want to learn to ride or even try overcome her fear?

"My mom's going to help Noah promote the rodeo school." Colton's pride was evident as he shared the news with Megan.

"That's cool," said his niece. "Because Uncle Noah is the best teacher ever." She reached her arms around his waist and squeezed him tight. "Right, Uncle Noah?"

He looked down at her. "If you say so, kid."

Megan released him then. "Come on, Colton. Let's go get some s'mores."

As the two trotted away, Lily smiled up at Noah. "The best teacher ever, huh?"

Heat crept up his neck. "If you believe an eleven-year-old."

She seemed to contemplate him for a moment. "You really think you can help me overcome my fear?"

"I do."

"In that case…" She held out her hand. "I think you've got yourself a deal."

Chapter Five

By the next morning, Lily was ready to back out of her deal with Noah. Sure, he might be good with horses, but did he really think he could help her overcome her fear?

Last night he'd said he could. But what if he couldn't? And what would her children think when they found out their mother was afraid of horses? Would they look at her differently? After all, she was supposed to take care of them. Protect them. Would they wonder what else she might be afraid of or think she's a coward?

Lily shook the torturous thoughts away and concentrated on the pancakes she was making for breakfast. Because despite her agreement with Noah, she still didn't have enough information to contact even a local newspaper regarding an interview. What she needed was a good hook that would make everyone in the state, if not the country, want to interview Noah and learn about the rodeo school. The only way to come up with that hook was to dig and find out what made Noah tick and why the rodeo school was so important to him.

After dotting one side of the pancakes with blueberries, she flipped them. They gently sizzled as the fruity aroma reached her nose, awakening her appetite.

Spatula in hand, she waited. How had Noah managed to turn the tables on her so easily last night? Not that he'd distracted her. It was being around all those horses that had made it difficult to think about anything except getting bitten or trampled, leaving her stammering and unable to concentrate.

She couldn't allow that to happen today. If only there was some way to get Noah away from the stable.

Maybe they could all go to lunch. Lily, Noah and the kids. Or better yet, she could pack a lunch for all of them. They could have a picnic at the park. It was supposed to be another beautiful day, and the views from the park were positively breathtaking.

Of course, if he was as busy today as he had been yesterday...

No, she was going to remain optimistic. If God wanted her to talk with Noah, He'd pave the way.

Armed with renewed determination, she loaded Colton and Piper into the SUV and set off for the ranch well before the rising sun broke over the mountain hugging the eastern edge of town. Colton had a job to do, and she would not allow him to be late. She wanted to instill a sense of responsibility while he was still young.

When they arrived, Colton ran on to start cleaning stalls while she and Piper found Noah sitting at the desk in the office, his back to them as he attached consent forms to clipboards.

She watched him curiously. "Why don't you have somebody to do that for you?" He was busy enough without a lot of little tasks consuming his time.

Only when he jerked his head in her direction did she realize that she'd probably startled him.

"Sorry. I should have knocked or at least said hello first."

"Nah." Wearing his usual jeans, work shirt and boots, he stood, sending his chair rolling across the concrete floor. "Actually, you're just the person I was hoping to see."

"A kitty." Piper spotted the calico sprawled atop the desk.

Noah glanced her way. "That's Patches." He looked at Lily then. "She's harmless."

Lily looked up at him. "Why were you hoping to see me?"

"What are you and the kids doing for lunch today?"

Her hand went to her hip. "Okay, that's weird, because I was going to ask you the same thing."

"No kidding?" He continued into the lobby with an armload of clipboards.

She followed him, determined that she would have the information she needed by the end of the day. "Yes. I was thinking that, since it's going to be another pretty day, we could have a picnic lunch at the park."

"Hmm…" He slid each clipboard over a hook on the rustic wooden wall. "That does sound like a good plan." Task complete, he faced her. "However, I know of someplace better than the park. And with a lot fewer people."

She like the sound of that. Less chance of being interrupted. "Wonderful. Where?"

"You'll just have to wait to find out."

"Seriously?"

"Do I look like I'm kidding?"

No, he definitely did not. She simply preferred to know these things so she could plan accordingly.

"You're just going to have to trust me, Lily."

Her gaze shot to his. Trust wasn't something that came easy to her. One of the downsides to being wealthy. People always expected something from her.

It's only lunch.

Yes, it was. A picnic at that.

"All right. I'll be here at noon with the food."

"What's on the menu?" Cowboy hat tilted back, Noah lifted a brow.

She sent him a smirk. "I guess you'll just have to trust *me*."

When she and Piper returned at noon, an excited Colton met them out front.

Under a cloudless sky, he rushed to the driver's-side door, all smiles, as she pressed the button to roll the window down.

With no sign of Noah, she wondered if there was a problem. Had he gotten busy again and needed to cancel? Then again, her son wouldn't be smiling if that were the case.

"Guess what, Mom?"

"What is it?"

"Noah said we get to ride to our picnic spot."

Lily found herself at a loss for words. Ride? As in a horse?

And to think, Noah actually had the nerve to tell her to trust him. As if simply putting her on a horse was going to help her get over her fear.

When the tall cowboy emerged from the building a moment later and came alongside her son, she was fit to be tied.

"I was telling them the good news." Colton was beyond excited. "That we get to ride horses to our picnic spot."

Lily remained silent behind her sunglasses, though that didn't stop her from glaring at Noah.

"Now let's not get too excited here." While Noah appeared to address all of them, those dark eyes remained fixed on her. "Colton is only partially right."

Lily waited for him to continue, fearful she might say something she shouldn't.

"The *kids* can ride while you and I take old Duke for a walk."

"Who, or should I say what, is Duke?" *Lord, please let it be a dog.*

"He's my horse."

"Of course he is." She undid her seat belt, killed the engine and rolled up the window before opening the door.

Noah backed out of the way as she moved to the rear of the vehicle to retrieve the basket of food. "Since it's such a nice day, I thought this would be the perfect opportunity for him to get out of the stable for a while. Away from the other horses."

She paused, her hand on the button to close the hatch. "He doesn't like the other horses?"

"Nah." He waved off her concerns. "They don't bother him. He just likes a little freedom now and then."

Lily swallowed against the tightness in her throat. "Then I guess you guys had better bring those horses out so we can be on our way." She glanced at Noah. "To wherever that may be."

"Great. The horses are already saddled, so, kids, if you will follow me."

Before he walked away, Lily said, "I do have one request."

"What's that?"

Head cocked, she clutched both hands around the basket handle. "Actually, it's more of a demand."

His gaze narrowed.

"That I do not leave here today without the information I need to move forward."

The corners of his mouth tilted upward. "You got it."

A few minutes later, Piper came around the side of the stable on a black-and-white Shetland pony, followed by Colton on the chestnut-colored horse he used for his lessons and—

"Oh, my."

Noah led his horse toward her.

Her head tilted back as she took in the massive black animal.

"Isn't Duke like the most awesome horse you've ever seen, Mom?" Colton beamed from atop his horse.

"He's *giant*." Piper stretched her arms as high as they would go.

"He is that." Lily took a step back.

When she did, the animal looked down at her with big black eyes. Her knees began to shake. Her pulse raced, and she felt like that frightened four-year-old girl again.

"I'll take this." Noah grabbed the picnic basket from her hands and tugged on the reins. "Come on, gang. Let's go."

They walked up the drive, past the barn and the house and into the pasture where cattle grazed in the distance. All the while, Lily made sure to keep a safe stretch of grass between herself and Duke.

"You know, Lily—" Noah looked her way, which was about eight to ten feet right of where he walked "—it makes it kind of hard to carry on a conversation when you're all the way over there. I mean, do you hear how loud I'm having to talk?"

She marched through the high grass. "I didn't want Duke to feel crowded."

"Don't you worry about Duke. You're not gonna bother him."

Maybe not, but he certainly bothered her.

A familiar sound touched her ears then. "Do I hear the river?"

"You sure do." A smiling Noah picked up the pace. "It's also our picnic spot."

"Awesome!" Colton fist-pumped the air.

Piper clapped. "Yay!"

Drawing closer, Lily could see it for herself. The way the Uncompahgre stretched to their right and left, winding as it went. The mountains in the distance were the perfect backdrop, with only the slightest slivers of snow still clinging to their peaks.

While the kids dismounted and Noah tethered their horses, Lily closed her eyes, stretched her arms wide and allowed the sun's warmth and the sound of rushing water to wash away her worries. This place was absolutely perfect.

When she opened her eyes, Noah stood before her. "Did I disappoint?"

She couldn't help but smile. "Definitely not."

"Good. Now, if you don't mind—" he held up the basket "—I'd like to see if you kept your end of the bargain."

"I hope you like liverwurst." After the walk she'd just had with Duke, it was hard not to tease him.

"Liverwurst?" Noah's look of horror told her she'd achieved her goal.

"Oh, yes." She took the basket from him and set it on the ground in the shade of a large cottonwood tree. "It's one of my favorites." Lifting the basket lid, she pulled out a blanket, shook it open and spread it on the ground.

"Liverwurst?" He smoothed the edges, his face still contorted.

"Oh, wait." Finished, she stood and touched a finger to her chin. "We were out of liverwurst. I brought ham and cheese and pimento cheese sandwiches."

He looked at her, his expression blank. "You know, Lily, I'm a pretty levelheaded guy. But right now, I'd like nothing more than to toss you into that river." He poked a thumb over his shoulder.

She stiffened. Surely, he was just playing. "You wouldn't."

"No, but I'd like to."

She turned toward the water, where Colton and Piper were running back and forth. "Kids, come eat." Glancing over at Duke, who was happily eating the grass while his reins lay on the ground, she addressed Noah. "Aren't you afraid he'll wander away?"

"No."

Well, that was a bit disconcerting. However, as they ate and laughed, she felt herself relax, despite the animal's presence. And when the kids went off to play again, she knew she finally had her chance.

Kneeling, she neatly tucked the empty plastic containers into the picnic basket, daring a peek at the long-legged cowboy who had stretched out on the opposite corner of the blanket, eyes closed with his hands tucked behind his head. She'd never seen him so relaxed. Not that she'd ever seen him uptight, but he looked different. Peaceful.

Who could blame him? She took in their surroundings. She'd been privileged enough to travel the world, yet the more time she spent in Ouray, the more she realized how much she enjoyed the simple things.

She checked on her children one more time. Seeing that they were busy feeding the horses handfuls of grass, she said, "You awake over there?"

"Yes, ma'am." Noah lifted one eyelid. "Just waiting for you to start pelting me with questions."

"In that case…" She sat down and made herself comfortable. "What made you decide to start the rodeo school?"

Noah wasn't used to opening himself up to people. Unfortunately, if he didn't, Lily wouldn't be able to do her job. And there was nothing he wanted—needed—more than for the rodeo school to be a success. Which meant he'd better answer her question.

He rolled up on one elbow. "Rodeo is my passion. I've been in love with it and with horses my entire life. But more than that—" He paused, knowing he needed to choose his words carefully. Or just get to the point. "Those two things helped me heal after my wife died."

Lily's brow furrowed, and her shoulders drooped as though she felt his pain. "How did she die?"

It had been a long while since Noah had talked about Jaycee's death. Though it was never far from his mind. He'd never forget walking into their cabin and finding her unconscious on the floor. He never got to talk to her again.

Not that he was going to share that with Lily. Still, if it hadn't been for Jaycee, he never would have even considered a rodeo school. Once upon a time, it had been her dream. She'd been a barrel-racing phenom, earning her own share of awards. At the time, he wasn't really interested in rodeo. Mostly because he didn't understand. Until she was gone and he experienced firsthand just how beneficial training and working with horses could be.

"She'd suffered a miscarriage. The doctors said later that she had developed an infection that turned into sepsis." If he had monitored her more closely, he might have seen the signs. Sure, she was sad, but he hadn't had a clue she was sick.

"I am so sorry, Noah. To go from the joy of expecting a child to losing both the baby and the woman you loved." She clenched a hand to her chest. "I can't begin to imagine how difficult that must have been for you."

"I had some pretty rough days. And ended up coping the only way I thought I could. By returning to the rodeo circuit and working 'round the clock. Practicing, trying new and different techniques, all in an effort to become the best rodeo champ ever."

Her smile was a sad one. "From what I've read, you succeeded."

"I suppose." Sitting up, he snagged a piece of grass. Rolled it between his fingers. "Course, it didn't hurt that I had a death wish. I figured I'd already lost everything..." He dropped the grass and looked her in the eye. "Which brings me to my second, more understated, reason for the rodeo school."

He twisted around to check on Colton, Piper and the horses. Assured that everyone was safe, occupied and a good distance from the river, he continued, "Rodeo, horses in particular, played a huge role in helping me work through the grieving process."

Hands clasped, she cocked her head, the breeze tossing tendrils of her long ponytail over her T-shirt–covered shoulder. "How so?"

"Not only are horses good listeners, they're very intuitive. They respond to the emotional state of those working with them."

"Meaning...?"

"We might think we're acting normal, but if we're grieving, impatient or angry, a horse will know and respond accordingly." He drew up one knee and hooked an arm around it. "While I don't want the rodeo school to be one of those therapy-type places, I'd eventually like to create an avenue to help kids dealing with grief."

"I have no doubt you would be very good at that. Just look at the changes you've brought about in Colton." Her troubled gaze drifted to her son. "This past year, he's had all sorts of behavioral issues." She looked at Noah again. "As you witnessed that first day when he tried to steal the horseshoes. But I've seen changes in him since he's been working with you."

"Why do you suppose he was acting out?"

She shrugged, eyeing a pair of birds chattering in the branches above. "I can't say for certain, but I think it has a lot to do with his father's lack of interest. Wade Davis doesn't have a lot of time for his children."

"Wait a minute." Noah dropped his leg and sat up straight. "Did you say Wade Davis?"

"Yes."

"The billionaire oilman?"

Her expression bordered on embarrassment. "That's the one."

Noah again looked for the kids as he tried to wrap his brain around that bombshell. Lily was married to Wade Davis? But she was so kind and unassuming, while Davis was an in-your-face, it's-all-about-me kind of guy. How on earth had those two ever gotten together?

He shook his head. "Doesn't he realize that his kids are the greatest treasure he could possess? That they're his legacy?"

"Unfortunately, no." She dusted crumbs from her gray T-shirt.

Noah watched the children as they took turns tossing rocks into the water. Colton and Piper were great kids. And their father ought to be ashamed of himself for turning his back on them. "I'm sorry, but your ex-husband has no idea what he's missing out on."

Following his gaze, she said, "I would have to agree."

He looked back at Lily. Saw the resignation in her eyes.

"Things don't always turn out the way we think they will, do they?"

He studied her a moment. "No, they don't." Pushing to his feet, he held out a hand to help her up. "But with your assistance, I'm sure the rodeo school will turn out even better than I imagined."

She smiled in earnest then. "I sure hope so."

"Come on." He nodded toward the river. "Let's go wrangle these kids so we can head on back."

"You two look like you're having fun," she said as they approached.

"Here, Mommy." Piper held out a well-rounded stone. "You need to skip a rock, too."

Her mother examined it. "Piper, honey, you need a flat rock for skipping." She eyed the water's edge. "Like this one." As she bent to pick it up, her foot slipped. "Ah!"

Noah reached out to catch her, but the grimace on her face said he was too late.

While she clutched her ankle, he hauled her back a few feet before crouching to her level. "How bad does it hurt?"

Her face contorted. "At the moment, pretty bad."

He carefully pulled off the low-heeled ankle-high boot and rolled up her skinny jeans as much as he could to discover that some swelling had already set in. "We're going to need to get some ice on this right away." Lifting his head, he let go a whistle.

"What was that for?" Lily's pain-filled eyes met his.

"Duke."

"Duke?"

"Yep." He stood as the horse came alongside them. "Good thing we let him come with us, because there's no way you're making it back to the house on your own."

Lily's gaze darted between him and Duke. "What do you mean?"

"It means that unless you want to be laid up for a week or more, Duke's gonna have to carry you back."

"Carry me?"

Noah would have had to be blind to miss the way Lily

glared at him, but there was no other choice. He had to get her back to the house and get some ice on her foot. "Well, I'm certainly not up to the task."

"It'll be okay, Mom." Colton laid a hand on his mother's shoulder. "Duke can handle it. He's a good horse."

"I'm sure he is, sweetheart, but I should be able to—" She struggled to stand until Noah reached out a helping hand. "See." She straightened. "I should have no problem—" One step was all it took and she was groaning again as her foot protested against the weight.

"Sorry, Lily, but it looks like Duke is your only ticket out of here."

Her nostrils flared. "Something I'm sure you're just thrilled about."

He took a step back. "You think I planned for you to get hurt?"

"No, but I'm sure you're enjoying this nonetheless."

He knew it was the pain talking, but that didn't mean he had to take it. "Look, I know we don't know each other very well, but I am not the kind of person who takes pleasure in other people's pain."

Her shoulders sagged again. "I'm sorry. I know you're trying to help me." She sent him a pleading gaze. "But isn't there another way?"

He eyed the kids. "You two go grab the basket and the blanket."

They took off without question.

Looking down at Lily's sad face, he wished he could accommodate her. But he couldn't.

"There is no other way, Lily. But I know that you can do this. You're a strong woman. And I'll be with you every step of the way."

Chapter Six

First she threw up in front of Noah, then she foolishly slipped and twisted her ankle. Could she possibly embarrass herself any more?

Lying on the lounge chair on the wooden deck of her cabin, Lily stared up at the leaves fluttering in the trees. Then to be forced to ride a horse… While Duke had been gentle enough, the only thing that had kept her from going into full-blown panic mode was knowing that her children were right there watching her.

She shook her head. At least nothing was broken.

Once they'd made it back to the stable yesterday, Clint drove her to the medical clinic in Ridgway for an X-ray, despite her insistence that she could drive herself. After all, she didn't need her left foot to drive. Of course, walking was another matter. After Dr. Lockridge determined it was only a sprain, he wrapped her ankle and sent her home with a pair of crutches and instructions to keep it iced and to stay off it unless absolutely necessary for at least two days. Longer if it still hurt.

She smiled thinking about Clint and the entire Stephens family. He'd brought her and the kids straight home, telling her they'd deliver her car later since she wouldn't be needing it. Then Carly and Lacie, Noah's sisters-in-law, brought dinner for her, Colton and Piper, while Jude, an Ouray police officer, was so kind to stop by and tell her he was working the night shift, then gave her his cell number in case she needed anything. Later, Noah had showed up, bearing ice cream and an apology for not taking her to the clinic himself. As if he needed to do that. The guy was busy enough without having to worry about her. Still, it felt good to know that someone cared.

The Stephens family was one loving and giving bunch. She wasn't sure she'd ever experienced anything quite like them before. Certainly not from her own family. Well, except for her grandma Yates.

Now, as she contemplated pizza delivery for tonight's meal and waited for Clint to return with Colton and Piper—he'd picked them up earlier and taken them to the ranch for their lessons—she read over the notes she'd made on her tablet, realizing she'd had a rather productive day. She'd researched the media outlets she wanted to contact for interviews, worked up a rough draft of the press release and jotted down multiple ideas for the grand opening event itself. Amazing what she could accomplish when she was forced to be still.

Just then, she heard gravel crunching under tires. She checked her watch. Ten after six. Anticipating Clint with the kids, she closed her tablet, grabbed her crutches and carefully made her way back into the house. By the time she arrived at the front door, she heard the sound of footsteps on the wooden stairs outside and Piper chatting excitedly about something.

Her heart stammered when she opened the wood, iron and glass door to discover Noah escorting her kids, a large brown paper sack dangling from each hand.

"We brought dinner," announced Piper.

"That's a pleasant surprise." Suddenly wishing she was wearing something other than sweatpants and a baggy T-shirt, she stepped out of the way to allow them entry.

"It's enchilada night at Granny's Kitchen." He gestured to the bags, his biceps straining the sleeves of his T-shirt. "We've got enchiladas, beans, rice, chips, salsa…"

The aromas had her stomach rumbling. "Sounds delicious." She closed the door and led him into the well-appointed galley kitchen. "Will you be joining us?"

Setting the bags on the granite countertop, he grinned. "I was hoping you'd ask."

While he emptied the bags of their foil to-go containers, she leaned one crutch against the counter, opened the cupboard and took hold of four plates.

"I'll get those." He intercepted her and set the plates on the counter.

Frowning, she cast him a sideways glance. "I'm not helpless, you know."

He looked down at her. "I do. However, my mother raised me to be a gentleman."

Heat crept into her cheeks. "She'd be very proud of you then." She moved to the silverware drawer. "I'm glad you're here, actually. There are several things I'd like to go over with you."

"Such as?" He removed the lids of the containers.

"Just some ideas for the rodeo school."

"Oh, so you weren't just sitting around, eating bonbons today."

She gathered knives and forks. "Sitting around, yes. Bonbons, no. Instead, I took the opportunity to go to work for you." Shoving the drawer closed with her hip, she eyed him again. "So if you could hang around a bit, I'll show you what I came up with."

"Not a problem, since Dad'll be bringing my truck by.

Oh—" he reached into the pocket of his jeans "—here are your keys." He held them out. "I parked your SUV in the drive, but I can put it in the garage if you prefer."

"No, the drive is fine." She set the silverware atop the plates and reached for the keys. Her fingers brushed against the palm of his hand, sending warmth through her fingertips, straight up her arm and directly to her heart. Try as she might, she couldn't remember a time in her life when someone had been so kind to her.

Closing her fist around the keys, she stepped back, refusing to read too much into it. Noah was a kind man. It was the way he was raised, and that's all there was to it.

After they'd finished their meal, the kids opted for a movie while Lily and Noah relaxed on the deck to go over her notes.

Sitting on the same chaise where she'd spent most of her day, she brought up the first page on her tablet. "This is a list of media outlets I plan to send press releases to. I believe we should get at least two or three interviews out of this. Some by phone, perhaps."

In the lounge chair beside her, he seemed to squirm. "About those interviews. I'm not real comfortable talking with reporters. Even when I was on the circuit."

Of course he wasn't. Noah wasn't the kind to brag or talk about himself. "I understand. Which is why we'll be sure to keep the focus on the rodeo school. But let's face it, if you wanted to further your career, whatever that may be, would you rather take lessons from someone who's dabbled in the field or a seasoned pro?"

"The pro, of course. But what if the interview turns personal?" He folded his hands atop his stomach. "I'm not planning to tell everyone what I told you yesterday."

"Noah." She set her tablet on her lap and faced him. "What you shared with me was to give me a better understanding of you so I can figure out how best to promote the school. And I'm glad you told me, because I think that propelled my work today."

"But what if they ask personal questions?"

"And they're apt to, believe me." She caught his horrified stare. "Sorry. I guess I've dealt with too many society columnists. Especially after Wade and I split. Speculations, accusations…" Resting her head against the back of the chair, she saw the first stars in the sky.

"What really happened?" He leaned closer. "Between you and Wade."

She studied him, realizing Noah was someone she could confide in and trust to keep the story to himself. "Honestly, things began to change when I started going to church again after a rather long absence. He said I wasn't *fun* anymore." Lifting a shoulder, she continued, "Things came to a head when my mother passed away. We were in Salt Lake City. Wade left right after the funeral because he had to get back for business reasons." She eyed her clasped hands. "At least that's what he said. But when I came home a day earlier than he expected, I found him in bed with another woman—who also happened to be my best friend."

Noah let go a sigh. He reached for her hands and gave them a squeeze. "Lily…"

She savored the comforting touch.

"I always think no one can understand what I went through after Jaycee died. But I have a feeling you get it better than anyone."

"To a point, yes." She faced him. "And having a recording device shoved in front of your face when you're going through something like that doesn't make things any easier."

"Sounds like you've had a lot of experience."

"More than I ever wanted, that's for sure." Which meant she might be able to help him. Releasing his hand, she sat up straighter. "What if I coached you? Gave you some tips on how to direct the interview to your advantage instead of letting them lead you."

He studied the night sky, pondering the suggestion. Nodded slowly. "I like that idea." He met her gaze. "I'll help you overcome your fear of horses and you help me conquer the interview."

"We'll be unstoppable," she teased.

"You got that right." He smiled.

Looking up at the stars, she let go a laugh. "Look out, world, here we come."

Lily was not the woman Noah had thought she was.

Two days after dinner at her place, he eased Duke from the rocky trail that wove down the side of the mountain into the grass-covered pasture, glancing over his shoulder to make sure the five riders behind him were still doing all right. Lily wasn't just any city girl. Thanks to a little internet research of his own, he'd discovered was a socialite. Born into wealth, married wealth... She was Colorado's version of those rich women you see in magazines. Yet she seemed so...normal.

With a warmer-than-usual midday sun overhead, he continued toward the stable. Saturdays were historically one of their busier days for trail rides. People came into Ouray for the weekend, looking for a change in scenery, an escape from city life or both. Like Lily. Only she was ready to escape for the entire summer.

He shifted in the saddle, the leather creaking. "Everyone doing okay back there?"

"We're doing *great*," said the young girl whose enthusiasm reminded him of Piper.

"Except it's almost over." Her teenaged sister eyed the stable ahead.

Sad to say, her disappointment was music to his ears. "I take it you enjoyed yourself then."

"Yes, sir," they said collectively.

Scanning the mountains to the south that surrounded the town of Ouray, he wondered how Lily's foot was doing. Thanks to an AWOL employee, yesterday had been another busy one, so he hadn't had a chance to stop by and see her. Not that he needed to. Still, there was a part of him that felt responsible for her sprained ankle. If they'd gone to the park as she'd suggested…

He waved off an annoying fly. Most people who lived in Colorado had at least heard of Wade Davis, the outspoken businessman who'd inherited a nice chunk of change from his late father, then gone on to accumulate his own fortune in the oil industry. Davis was a man who loved the limelight. And Lily had been married to him.

Tilting his hat back, Noah scratched his head. For the life of him, he still couldn't figure that one out. Davis and Lily were as different as night and day.

Not so unlike you and Jaycee. True. Yet while Jaycee had been content to live a simple life, her family had always looked down on him, even going so far as to blame him for her death. His chest tightened. Wasn't it enough that he blamed himself?

He shook off the unwanted memories, grateful they were approaching the stable.

After saying goodbye to his group, he took Duke around to the side of the building for a drink of water, then went inside to grab a bottle for himself. Savoring the cool air in the storage room, he tugged a rag from his back pocket and wiped the sweat off his neck, praying today's heat was just a fluke and not an indicator of what was to come.

His phone buzzed in his pocket. He pulled it out to see the name Marshall Briggs on the screen. Marshall was an old friend from his rodeo days, but he hadn't talked to the fella in at least two years.

He pressed the button and put the phone to his ear. "Hey, Marshall. How's it going?"

"Not too good, I'm afraid."

The muscles in Noah's shoulders knotted. "Why? What's up?"

The man who'd been one of Noah's mentors let out a breath. "You haven't heard about Cody, have you?"

"Chandler?" Noah had mentored the up-and-coming kid, who now appeared to be ready to shatter some, if not all, of Noah's records. "No. What about him?"

"Bull got the best of him in Reno last night."

Noah blinked a few times, knowing what his friend was saying, yet not wanting to believe it. "Is he…?" He couldn't bring himself to say the word.

"Late last night."

Running a hand over his face, he sank into one of two wooden chairs near the door. Set his water bottle on the concrete floor. Cody was the best of the best. He had a wife, a new baby… "What happened? Cody was setting up to be an all-round world champ."

"He hesitated. Bull got to him before he could get up." Marshall paused. "You know as well as I do that there's a risk every time we head out there."

Yes, but that didn't make things any easier. Especially when it was someone so young and yet so experienced.

His mentor continued, "Best we can do is pray for his family and know that he died doing what he loved."

Cody might have been doing what he loved, but Noah

had no doubt that Cody's wife held her breath each and every time he burst out of that chute. Just like Jaycee had done with him. Until they decided to have a family, anyway. He'd walked away then, disappointed yet unaware his retirement would be so short-lived.

He cleared his throat. "How is Cheryl holding up?"

"Not so good."

Tossing his hat onto the stainless steel work table, Noah shoved a hand through his hair. He knew exactly how Cheryl felt. As though her heart had shattered into so many tiny fragments it could never be put back together. Like the simple act of breathing was suddenly too much. And feeling the burn of anger and wanting to rail at God for taking away your reason for getting up in the morning.

His eyes fell closed. He pinched the bridge of his nose. *God, be with her as only You can.* "Any word on funeral arrangements?"

"Not yet. I'll keep you posted, though."

"Thanks, Marshall." He ended the call and leaned his head against the wall. As he stared up at the wooden rafters, one question played through his mind. Why? It was a question he'd asked hundreds of times before. Now here it was again. And while he didn't have an answer, he knew Marshall was right. With bull riding, there were no guarantees. Unlike most jobs, you challenged death every time you went off to work. This time, Cody wasn't coming home.

"There you are."

He jumped at the sound of Lily's voice. Scrambled to his feet. "You're here."

"I am." Leaning on her crutches, she looked at him suspiciously.

"Did you drive? Aren't you supposed to be resting?" His rapid-fire questions surprised even him.

"Foot's better. Yes, I drove. I'm still taking it easy, but I wanted to tell you—" She tilted her head. "Are you all right, Noah? You look like you're upset." She was on to him.

He couldn't let that happen.

He did his best to shrug off Marshall's phone call. "Naw, I'm not upset." He stooped to pick up his water bottle and uncapped the lid. "A little overheated, that's all." He took a drink. "Just got back from a trail ride."

"Ah." With her fingers wrapped around the handgrips of her crutches and her bad foot lifted slightly, she straightened. "That makes sense. It's toasty out there today."

"Especially when you're on top of a horse and there's no shade." He took another drink, emptying the bottle. "I guess the ankle's feeling better?"

"Much."

"You should still sit down, though." He motioned for her to take the seat he'd just vacated.

"I'm okay. Really."

"Where are the kids?"

"Your father talked them into joining him for a Popsicle."

He felt the corners of his mouth lift. "I'm guessing he didn't have to do much talking, did he?"

"No, not at all."

He grabbed another water. "Want one?"

"No, thank you."

He unscrewed the lid. "You wanted to talk to me?"

"Yes." Again, she watched him, as though knowing something wasn't right. "I heard back from one of the media outlets I contacted. The *Denver Post*, no less."

An hour ago, he would have been impressed. Now?

"They're going to be in the area and would like to set

up an interview with you for this coming week. Tuesday, preferably."

"That soon, huh? You must have really sold them."

"Well, that is part of my job."

"Yeah." Except when he'd brought her on board, Cody was still alive. Now he was gone. How could Noah think about, let alone talk about, teaching others—young people, no less—to put their lives on the line in the name of fun? Because it wasn't always fun. Cody and Cheryl had learned that the hard way. And neither Cheryl nor her child would ever be the same.

Chapter Seven

Lily awoke frustrated Sunday morning. Something was bothering Noah. And whatever it was had kept him from giving her a definitive answer on that interview.

Her irritation grew as she stirred the eggs in the skillet. She understood that he was busy. However, time was not on their side. Saturday would be July Fourth. Meaning there were only two months left until Labor Day. Not to mention she had to be back in Denver by August 15. If Noah wanted this grand opening to be a success, he needed to stop dragging his feet.

She scooped a serving of scrambled eggs onto a plate. "Colton. Piper. Breakfast."

Today wasn't about Noah, though. Or the ranch. This was Sunday. A day of rest and worship. Even if they were on vacation—albeit an extended one—they still needed to have their spiritual tanks filled. That meant going to church. And afterward, they were going to drive down to Ironton, an abandoned mining town one of the locals had told her about. The kids seemed eager to check it out. They were already asking if they could pan for gold in the river.

"Thanks, Mom," said Colton, taking his plate. To her surprise, he hadn't balked or argued when she woke him up. She was pleased with the changes she'd seen in him since he'd been working at the ranch. He was more respectful and seemed to have a good work ethic. Thanks to Noah.

She spooned eggs onto Piper's plate, wondering, yet again, what was troubling Noah. Because she highly doubted it was the heat, as he'd claimed.

Since her ankle wasn't one hundred percent, they drove to Restoration Fellowship, a small brick church she'd been eyeing on their nightly walks around town. Still using her crutches so as not to risk putting too much weight on her bad foot, Lily made her way with the kids up the walk, past a large fir tree, to the solid wooden doors where an older gentleman awaited them.

"Welcome to Restoration Fellowship."

"Thank you." She hobbled past the man, taking in the narrow foyer. "It's nice to be here." Especially since she'd missed worship services the past two weeks. She glanced up the long, dead-end hallway.

The older man must have sensed her confusion, because he said, "Just make a left midway down the hall, and the sanctuary will be straight ahead."

When they rounded the corner, there were two more gentlemen carrying on a conversation. The closest one, a very tall man with thick, dark hair, had his back to her.

The shorter man facing them paused, smiled and said, "Welcome to Restoration Fellowship."

The tall man turned their way. "Good morn—"

"Noah?" Colton's expression went from moderate interest to full-blown excitement.

"Hey, guys." Noah scanned the three of them. And though he wore a hint of a smile, whatever had been bothering him yesterday still lingered in the lines that creased his brow.

"What are you doing here?" Piper stared up at him, looking somewhat perplexed.

"This is where I attend church." His attention shifted to Lily then, and she took a step back. This was not the cowboy she was used to seeing. The man standing before her now, sporting a pair of stone khakis and a tailored, untucked blue shirt that complemented his physique as well as his eyes, had her a little off-kilter. "I'm glad you could join us."

"Well, look who we have here?" Clint's voice sent the kids' excitement level even further up the scale.

Lily turned to see him approach with a stylishly dressed Hillary at his side, once again raising Lily's suspicions that the two were more than just friends. Not that there was anything wrong with that. Clint was a widower. His children were grown. Why shouldn't he be allowed to find love again?

Her children hung on the older man's every word as he told them how long he'd been coming to this church and how happy he was to see them here.

"Dad, you're creating a bottleneck." Noah motioned to the people waiting behind them.

"Hmm." The older man jerked toward the people in question. "Sorry 'bout that." He took hold of Piper's hand and nodded for Colton. "Let's go get us a seat."

Next thing Lily knew, she and her children were in a cushioned pew, surrounded by the entire Stephens clan, except for Carly, who was holding down the fort at her bed-and-breakfast. Not exactly what Lily had envisioned when she woke up this morning. Especially the good-looking man sitting on the other side of Piper.

Still, the pastor's message about how God uses all things for good struck a chord. While her life had been a privileged one, she'd known her share of difficulties. Yet, now she was able to look back and see how God used even some of the worst events in her life to not only grow and strengthen her, but to bring her to places she'd never expected.

Kind of like coming to Ouray. If it hadn't been for Colton's behavioral issues, she probably wouldn't have been so determined to get the kids away from Denver. As a result, Colton's bad attitude seemed to have disappeared. Her children were happier than she'd ever seen them.

Her gaze inadvertently drifted to Noah. He'd played a big role in those changes. And seeing him here today only bolstered her awareness.

Straightening, she again faced the pulpit. Good thing they already had plans for today. Because the last thing she needed was to find herself at the ranch, being bombarded with wayward thoughts. Her life and her children's lives were in Denver. Something that was not about to change anytime soon.

After the service, she met the pastor, then led her children outside as they again chatted with Clint. The sky was a gorgeous blue. Birds were singing. The sun was warm. A perfect day for exploring.

"Say—" with Hillary at his side, Clint clapped his hands together with a smile "—why don't you all come on out to the ranch today? We'll have lunch, and you can help us get the old farm wagon ready for the parade on Saturday."

Lily cringed.

"The Fourth of July parade?" Colton's green eyes sparkled.

"That's the one," said Clint. "You kids planning to attend?"

They nodded eagerly.

"Mom showed us a book with a bunch of pictures," said Colton. "I can't wait to see the fire-hose fights."

"Oh, you don't want to miss those." Clint nudged his cowboy hat—one that was far more pristine than the one he wore at the ranch.

Lily was still trying to come up with a polite way to bow out when Noah approached with his brothers Jude and Daniel.

"What's going on?" He eyed his father as if he knew he was up to something.

"Lily and the kids are going to join us for lunch."

She nearly choked. She hadn't agreed. Nor did she plan to.

"Clint Stephens—" Hillary elbowed him "—you're getting ahead of yourself again. Poor Lily hasn't been able to get a word in edgewise to say if they will or won't be joining us."

"He has a habit of doing that." Noah glared at his father.

The older man looked embarrassed. "Sorry, Lily. The kids and I got a little excited talking about the parade."

"That's all right, Clint." Not that he wasn't making it extremely difficult for her to say no. Especially with her kids staring up at her with those hopeful expressions. "I thought you kids wanted to go to Ironton today and do some exploring."

"That was before Mr. Stephens invited us," said Colton.

"Please, Mommy," Piper begged.

How was she supposed to say no to that?

"I guess we could do Ironton another day." She squinted against the sun. "But what about the trail rides?"

"Closed on Sundays," said Clint.

She nodded. Maybe the wagon would be outside or at the barn instead of the stable. In which case, she really would enjoy helping. After all, a small-town Fourth of July parade was one of those simple pleasures she wanted her children to participate in.

Again, she looked at her kids. Their wide eyes full of expectation. As far as they were concerned, a new adventure awaited. And she couldn't say no to that.

Her gaze drifted to Noah.

No matter how badly she might want to.

Noah wasn't in the mood for company, let alone participating in something that was supposed to be fun. Instead, he wanted to escape from everyone and everything. Yet here he was, on the deck of the ranch house, the aromas of grilling meat wafting around him as he listened to the happy chatter of Lily, Colton, Piper, Hillary and his family, while he barely held it together. Didn't they realize that the news about Cody still had him in a tailspin?

Of course they didn't. Because he never told them.

Dad offered up a brief prayer before telling everyone to come and get some food. As usual, his father manned the grill while Hillary, Carly and Lacie saw to all of the side dishes.

Noah peered at the spread, surprised. Was that barbecued chicken? Dad always served beef.

His gaze drifted to Hillary. She must've encouraged the old cattle rancher to stop being so stuck in his ways.

Falling in line behind Lily at the food table at the far end of the deck, Noah couldn't help noticing the way she tried to balance a crutch with one hand and her plate with the other. And though he didn't want to help, didn't want to interact or do anything else that might encourage her to start up a conversation, his mother had taught him to do what was right.

"Let me help you with that." He took hold of her plate. "Just tell me what you want, and I'll get it for you."

She looked up at him, surprise darting back and forth in her green eyes.

He supposed he couldn't blame her. Not when he'd barely said two words to her all day. Throw in his behavior yesterday and—

"Thank you," she finally said.

When both of their plates were full, they sat with Piper at one of the picnic tables while Colton joined Megan.

"I really enjoyed the service today." Lifting a forkful of her broccoli salad, Lily watched Noah suspiciously across the table. As though she knew something wasn't right.

"Me, too." He inched farther under the shade of the table umbrella, glad he'd forced himself to go this morning. The uplifting and encouraging message was just what he needed. Even if he couldn't imagine any good that could possibly come out of Cody's or Jaycee's deaths.

Though Lily didn't say any more, he could feel her gaze probing him, looking for answers as to why he was being so standoffish. Not that it was any of her business.

Why do you feel guilty then?

Because he had yet to give her an answer on that interview. How could he, though, when, as of right now, he wasn't even certain he wanted to proceed with the rodeo school? Not after yesterday.

What about all your plans? Your dream? You put your savings into that arena. Are you going to let it all go?

His passion had definitely waned. And right now he wasn't sure he'd ever get it back.

"Everyone, make sure you save room for dessert." Dad took a seat beside him as Hillary eased next to Piper.

"So, Clint—" Lily wiped her hands on a paper napkin "—is that the wagon you're planning to decorate?" She pointed to the old farm wagon sitting across the way, beside the barn.

"Sure is." His father cut a bite of chicken and shoved it in his mouth.

"Have you always used it in the parade?"

"For the last few years we have." Dad reached for his water cup. "It's a way to advertise the trail rides."

"I see." Lily set her plasticware atop her nearly empty plate. "In that case, why don't you consider using it to advertise the rodeo school instead?"

"Hadn't thought about that." His father tore a slice of bread in half. "Sounds like a good idea, don't you think, Noah?"

He chewed his last bite of chicken, his irritation growing. He didn't want to be here. Didn't want to think about advertising of any sort. What he wanted was to saddle Duke and find a quiet place in the woods where he could be alone to collect his thoughts. "I guess."

"That reminds me." Lily shoved her plate out of the way. "Do you have a website?"

Noah shrugged when his father deferred to him. "A basic one for the trail rides and riding school. Hours, contact info…"

"Nothing for the rodeo school?" Her brow puckered as she continued to watch him.

"No." Unable to look at her, he focused on the half-eaten pile of coleslaw on his plate. A few days ago, he might have benefited from this conversation. But things were different now.

"Not even some info on the existing website?"

He shook his head and blew out a breath, longing to escape. He wasn't in the mood to talk business.

"In that case, I highly recommend that you have a separate website for the rodeo school. And that you get it up and running ASAP. If we're advertising, people need to know where they can go to get more information."

Tension clamped down on his shoulder muscles. "Look, it's hard enough managing the basic website we have. I don't have time to come up with another one. Let alone in six days."

"I get that, Noah."

His gaze darted to hers, as though longing for someone to understand. He didn't want to let anybody down. However, the thought of moving forward with rodeo school, something that only yesterday he'd been eagerly anticipating, now terrified him.

She continued, "But in today's world, you can't just hang out a sign and expect people to come running. An internet presence is vital."

"Lily has a good point." Hillary wiped her fingers. "I know that whenever I hear of something that interests me, the first thing I do is look the business up on the internet."

"You would." Dad frowned.

Hillary glared back. "I may be a middle-aged grandmother, but I'm still one hip chick."

"Middle-aged?" His father lifted a brow. "You planning on living till you're a hundred and twenty?"

His sparring partner sent him a smug grin. "If not longer." She returned her attention to Lily and Noah. "I'm not an expert in web design, but I am rather tech savvy. I keep up the website for Granny's Kitchen and even redesigned it a few months ago. I'd be happy to come up with a website for the rodeo school."

"Hillary, that'd be great." Lily's enthusiasm only amplified Noah's agitation. "We could get some pictures from Noah's rodeo days, a bio…"

Sweat beaded his brow.

"That's a great idea, Lily. Could you help me come up with ideas for the content?"

His heart thundered against his chest.

"Absolutely."

Fists balled, he pushed to his feet, his breathing ragged. "Enough!"

Looking around, he saw everyone staring at him. His brothers, sisters-in-law, nieces…Lily and her children.

He'd lost control. Something he hadn't done in a very long time. And he owed them an explanation.

"There's not going to be a rodeo school."

Chapter Eight

Lily's heart went out to the man standing in front of her, no matter how much she didn't want it to. This was her fault. She'd pushed too hard. Noah wasn't a businessman. He was a cowboy who loved horses and being outdoors. Her role was to help him. Instead, she'd driven him over the edge.

Clint stood. Laid a hand on his oldest son's shoulder. "What's got you so upset?"

Noah's eyes closed momentarily. When he opened them, he scanned the faces of his family before zeroing in on Lily. "If you'll please excuse me."

He turned then, the sound of his boots hollow against the wooden deck until he stepped to the ground and continued down the gravel drive toward the stable.

The lump in Lily's throat threatened to strangle her. The way Noah had looked at her. The pain and anguish in his eyes and the lines etched on his face. Why hadn't she noticed them earlier? Instead, she just kept hammering, as though the entire rodeo school hung on advertising and a website.

"What happened, Mommy?" Piper's blue eyes were filled with confusion, her bottom lip slightly pooched.

She wrapped an arm around her daughter. "Noah's just feeling a little overwhelmed, that's all." Except that wasn't all. She was certain of it.

Memories of yesterday moved through her mind. His strange behavior when she found him in the storage room. His features had been filled with distress. Much the way they'd been only moments ago.

Hillary inched closer. "You all right, honey?"

"Of course." Out of the corner of her eye, she saw Noah's niece Kenzie approach.

"Piper, want to play ponies with me?" The child pointed toward the other table and pile of colorful plastic horses.

Her daughter's eyes widened. "Can I, Mommy?"

"Sure, go ahead." She watched her walk away before returning her attention to Hillary. "Would you mind keeping an eye on my children? I need to apologize to Noah."

"Well, yes. If that's what you feel like you need to do." Warmth mingled with confusion in the older woman's deep brown eyes.

"I was rude. This was supposed to be a fun day, and I ruined it by talking business."

"You were just trying to help. We both were."

"Yes, but for all my help, I only succeeded in making him want to give up his dream." She stood. Took hold of her crutches. "I don't know how long I'll be gone."

"Doesn't matter. The kids'll be fine."

She passed Clint on her way off the deck.

"Where are you headed?"

Fearing he'd try to stop her, she kept moving. "To apologize to your son."

By the time she made it to the stable, she was ready to toss her crutches. They might take the pressure off her foot, but they sure slowed her down.

Inside, the smells of horse and hay gave her pause. She

had no idea where Noah was, but her first guess would be with Duke. That meant she had no choice but to head for the stalls.

Her palms began to sweat.

You're doing this for Noah.

With a bolstering breath, she headed down the main corridor before veering off at the row of stalls where they kept Duke.

Save for the occasional sound of horses, the place was silent.

"Noah?"

Somewhere farther down, a horse nickered. But there was no sign of Noah. Unless he was ignoring her. Continuing past the first two animals, she again called his name.

This time he appeared from Duke's stall. "What are you doing here?"

She moved toward him as fast as she could, though it felt like a snail's pace.

Stopping in front of him, she again noticed the deep lines etched in his brow. His drawn lips. And the unmistakable sorrow in his eyes.

"I wanted to apologize for being so tough on you back there."

Hands on his denim-clad hips, he watched her for a moment before looking away. "I'm a cowboy, not a china doll. I know what tough is, and trust me, you weren't tough."

"Then why would you give up your dream?"

He looked everywhere but at her then, not saying a word.

"You don't have to tell me," she finally said. "But I wish you would."

Still nothing. Not so much as a grunt. He just stood there, engrossed in the rafters, walls, horses, floor…

"Okay. I've made my apologies. I'll leave you alone."

She turned and started back up the aisle, disappointment weaving its way around her heart. *God, whatever's bothering Noah, please help him.*

"One of the cowboys I mentored—"

She turned at the sound of his voice. Moved toward him.

"Cody Chandler was his name."

"Was?"

He gave a slight nod. "He was killed in the arena Friday night."

Her body sagged with grief. For Cody, for Noah. "I'm so sorry."

"I haven't told anyone because I'm…conflicted."

"About?"

He stared at the overhead lights. "I taught Cody everything I know. Yet I'm still here and he's…"

Reaching for him, she squeezed his forearm.

He laid his free hand over hers as though welcoming the touch. "How can I teach others, knowing that they could end up like Cody?"

She chose her words carefully, knowing that nothing she could say would suddenly make things better. "You said Cody was killed in the arena. What does that mean, exactly?"

"Bull riding." He patted her hand before lowering his own. "He was thrown but didn't get out of the way in time."

Her insides cringed at the image that formed in her mind. He didn't need to tell her any more.

She cleared her throat. "I may have misunderstood, but I was under the impression that the rodeo school was more about horses and roping than bull riding."

"It is. But students will expect to be exposed to some bull riding."

"Can you use one of those mechanical bulls? You know, like in *Urban Cowboy.*"

Not only did the corners of his mouth tilt upward then, he actually grunted out a laugh. "*Urban Cowboy?* Seriously?"

"What? I figured that's how you guys trained."

"It is. But that's kind of an insult. I mean—" he stepped back, held his arms out "—do I look like John Travolta to you?"

She lifted a brow and pretended to study him. "Well, you do have dark hair."

"If it wasn't for that bum foot of yours, you just might find yourself on top of a horse right now."

Suddenly grateful for her klutziness, she dipped her head. "When I first asked you about the rodeo school, why you wanted to do it, you said that rodeo was your passion. That it had helped you and you hoped to use it as a means to help others dealing with grief. Has Cody's death changed all of that?"

He thought for a long moment. "No. I just don't want to encourage people to go out there, thinking it's all fun and games."

"First of all, that's not your MO." She leaned on her crutches. "I've seen the safety measures you take around here. How serious you are about training. But rodeo is a sport. And just like any other sport—football, baseball— there are risks. You know that. I'm sure Cody knew that."

A long moment ticked by before he said, "How'd you get so smart?"

"I'm simply reminding you of things you already know. The rest is up to you."

His nod said he understood. "How did you manage to make it down here, anyway? Past all these horses." He gestured up the aisle.

"Sheer determination, I guess."

"Because you thought you owed me an apology?"

"Yes, but now that I know you can take it…"

While he chuckled, she felt rather embarrassed.

"I need to go check on Colton and Piper." Turning, she again hobbled up the aisle, praying Noah would come to the decision that was right for him. That he would pursue God's will, whatever that may be.

Approaching the practice ring, she heard Noah call her name. She turned to see him jogging up behind her, smiling.

"Hey, would you mind letting that reporter know that Tuesday would be fine for an interview?"

Her grin was instantaneous. "Of course. But what about the coaching we discussed?"

"We've got two days. I'm ready and willing whenever you're able."

"Cody Chandler was killed over the weekend after being thrown from a bull." Duff Hinson, a sports reporter from the *Denver Post*, watched him intently, recording device in hand. "You mentored Cody. Is there anything you wish you would have told him? Anything that could have prevented this tragedy?"

Noah sucked in a breath, grateful to Lily for reminding him why he'd wanted the rodeo school in the first place. Not to mention the coaching she'd given him for this interview, preparing him for such a question.

"Cody's death is a tragedy, and my prayers go out to his wife, Cheryl, and their little girl. But rodeo is a sport that, just like any other sport, has its risks. Every cowboy knows that coming out of the chute. Yet, despite all of our training, life still happens. That's when we have to step back and remember Who's in control."

Duff lowered the recorder and smiled. "That should do it then." He tucked the device into his pocket. "Thank you, Noah." He shook his hand. "We'll just get a few photos and be out of your way."

The photographer took one of him with Duke in the arena.

"Can we get one of you instructing a student?" Duff eyed the staff that had gathered, but Noah had a better idea.

"Colton?" The boy had been sitting beside Lily, watching intently the entire time. "Is Sonic still saddled?"

The kid leaped to his feet. "Yes, sir."

"Why don't you grab him so we can give these fellas a demo?"

Colton was off like a flash.

He eyed one of his employees. "Jackie? Would you mind putting a calf in the pen?"

"You got it, boss."

Once everyone was in place, he walked through his plan with Colton. "I know you haven't practiced roping with a real calf yet, but for the sake of their pictures—" he nodded in the direction of the newspaper guys "—I'm going to let you give it try, okay?"

The boy looked skeptical. "I don't think I can do it."

"That's all right, I'm not expecting you to. They just want some pictures."

The kid's smile reappeared as determination squared his shoulders. "I'll do my best."

"That's all any of us can do," said Noah.

He watched as Colton walked toward the pen. Then cringed when he tripped and fell face-first into the dirt. "You okay?"

The boy hurried to his feet, face red, but still laughing. "Yeah."

Inside the pen, he climbed atop his horse. And though this was only for show, Noah couldn't help noticing how seriously Colton approached the challenge. He had his rope coiled perfectly. He eyed the calf in the next pen, then the arena.

Noah was rooting for the kid. There was a first time for everything, after all.

Finally, both pens opened, and Colton was off. He swung his rope. Sent it airborne.

Cheers erupted from onlookers, with Lily's being the loudest. He'd done it. Colton had roped his first calf.

Pride swelled in Noah's chest as he hurried toward the photographer. "I hope you got that."

"I did," the man said.

"Good, because I want a copy."

Colton practically flew from his horse. "Did you see that?" He rushed toward Noah, giving him a massive hug.

Leaning into the boy, he said, "You did great. I'm proud of you."

And when Colton stepped back, the look he gave Noah was unlike anything he'd seen before. A look that filled him with emotions he'd never known.

Lily rushed in to congratulate her son. "You did it!"

"Can I call Dad?" The boy watched her, expectant.

"Sure." She handed him her phone and waited as he dialed.

Finally, "Dad, guess what?" His smile faltered. "But it's important." A moment later he beamed. "I roped my first calf."

Lily's nervous gaze darted from Colton to Noah.

"That's it. Isn't that cool? I did it all by my—" His exuberance evaporated. "Well...yeah. I wanted—" A moment later Colton ended the call, thrust the phone toward his mother and sprinted across the arena.

Concern filled Lily's eyes. "I need to go after him." She pushed past Noah.

"You're not going alone." He was right behind her. "Dad," he hollered, "keep an eye on Piper."

With his father's thumbs-up behind him, he bypassed a hobbling Lily in the aisle and waited for her at the front door. "Any guesses what happened back there?"

She pushed up the sleeves of her lightweight sweater. "Yes. His father dismissed him once again."

Anger fueled Noah as he stepped into the bright sun. "You start here and work your way up to the house. I'll check the barn and the rest of the immediate area." Yet, when they met at the house a short time later, neither had seen hide nor hair of Colton.

Lily was beside herself. Her brow puckered with worry while a tear spilled onto her cheek. "Where could he have gone?"

He scanned the area around them. "I don't know." He met her gaze then. "However, I do know every square inch of this ranch." He gripped her shoulders. "We're going to find him."

She nodded quickly.

"You wait here or at the barn. I'm going to take the UTV and search the pastures. I'll call you just as soon as I know something."

"Okay." More nodding. "And I'll let you know if he shows up here."

He hurried to the utility vehicle they used to get around the ranch and fired up the engine. With one last glance toward Lily, he was off.

Where could Colton have gotten to so fast?

His grip tightened around the steering wheel. *God, please lead me.*

Moving through the pasture behind the house, he noticed a thin strip of recently flattened grass. He followed it into the woods, his gut tightening as he realized where it led. That's when he spotted Colton, sitting on the porch of the cabin Noah had shared with Jaycee.

He swallowed hard. In the past twelve years, he'd done little more than drive past the building. Even then, he didn't dare look.

Then he recalled Lily finding him in the stable the other day. Working her way past all those horses to get to him.

If she could face her fear, he could, too.

He killed the engine and sent Lily a text that said, Found him, before continuing up to the cabin.

He sat down beside Colton on the top porch step. "How did you manage to get out here so fast?"

The kid shrugged, refusing to look at him.

"Mind telling me why you ran off?"

Colton hung his head. "I wasn't mad at you guys. It was my dad."

"What about your dad?"

"He was too busy to listen to me."

A breeze rustled the leaves overhead.

"But I heard you tell him you roped your first calf."

The kid looked up at Noah then, his eyes swimming with tears. "He said, 'You called me for that?'" He lowered his voice to mimic his father. "And that he didn't have time for my nonsense." The tears fell then.

Noah's blood boiled. How could any parent treat a child that way? He understood busy, but surely the guy could have spared a minute or two for his son, especially when it was obvious how excited Colton was about his achievement.

"Perhaps you caught your father at a bad time." Was he really defending the guy?

"There's never a good time with him."

Noah wasn't sure he'd ever been this angry. No kid should feel this way, no matter how large your bank account. "You know, I've been thinking. How would you like to ride alongside me in the Fourth of July parade?"

Colton's head popped up. He sniffed and wiped at his face. "You mean, like, on my own horse?"

He nodded. "We'd need to check with your mama first, but you and Sonic have been getting on pretty good. You're becoming quite the horseman."

"I am?"

While Noah wasn't stretching any truths, he was amazed at what that little bit of encouragement did for the boy. Now he was beginning to understand why Colton had been so difficult when they'd first met.

"You sure are. All that practicing you've been doing has paid off. I'm proud of you." He didn't think the kid's grin could get any bigger, but it did. "However—" he stood "—your mother was quite worried about you, so we'd best get on back."

"Yeah. She worries a lot."

"That's because she loves you."

Another grin told him that Colton knew he was speaking the truth.

Turning to leave, Noah gave the log cabin a final once-over, noting how much it had deteriorated and feeling somewhat sad. A different kind of sad, like the place had been forgotten. Probably because he'd wanted to forget. After Jaycee's death, he came back here once, grabbed everything that didn't remind him of her and never darkened its door again.

He looked down at Colton. "How did you find this place?"

"I saw it on one of our rides. What is it, anyway?"

"It used to be someone's home."

The kid looked up at him. "Whose?"

"Mine."

"Why don't you live here now?"

How could he even begin to explain something he couldn't quite understand himself?

He placed an arm around the boy's shoulders. "That's a story for another day. Come on, your mother is waiting."

Chapter Nine

Colton was safe, and the Fourth of July had finally arrived.

Excitement bubbled inside Lily. Between the photos they'd seen and everything people had told them, she'd been anticipating this day for weeks. And her kids? The way they'd been counting down, one would think it was Christmas.

Today they'd get to experience Ouray at its best. From the parade to the fire-hose fights to the fireworks and everything in between.

Standing on the front porch of Carly and Andrew's historic bed-and-breakfast Saturday morning, Lily was grateful that, for this one day, she wouldn't have to worry about going to the ranch. Not that she didn't like the ranch. On the contrary, she found it quite beautiful. Especially that spot near the river where Noah had taken them for their picnic that day. That was, before she went and ruined everything by twisting her ankle.

Now that her foot had healed, though, she knew it was only a matter of time before Noah would decide to execute his plan to help her overcome her fear. And she didn't want the possibility of having to ride a horse hanging over her head and ruining her good time today.

"You have a beautiful home, Carly." While Piper hurried down the porch steps, Lily gave the gracious Victorian a final once-over before starting down the front walk.

"Thank you." Noah's sister-in-law absently laid a hand atop her growing baby bump. "As I like to say, Granger House Inn isn't just our home, she's a member of the family."

Lily pressed a hand to her chest as she met the woman's gray-blue gaze. "Oh, I love that." She again surveyed the sea-foam-green house with its large porch and intricate millwork. "I hope you use that line in your promotional material."

Carly smiled as they continued into the yard. "Ever since the fire I have." During their tour, she'd told Lily about the fire that had ravaged a portion of the home early last year. Something that had ultimately brought her and Andrew together.

The nicker of a horse drew Lily's attention to the next drive, where Colton and Megan sat atop their respective steeds. Noah had decked the kids out with boots, chaps and Stetsons, making them look as though they'd come straight from the rodeo. Perfect advertising.

Noting the grin on Colton's face, Lily thought back to Tuesday evening when Noah returned with him after he'd bolted from the stable. While she'd been scared to death, her son was beside himself with excitement, begging her to let him ride with Noah in the parade. As if she could have said no. Not when she was so happy to see him. However, learning of how his father had treated him had her wanting to wring Wade Davis's neck.

Her gaze drifted to Noah, who was sitting tall in his saddle. They'd only known him a couple of weeks, yet he'd taken the time to listen to Colton. And then, later, let her know in no uncertain terms that he was not happy with her ex.

Those are his children, he'd said. *They deserve to be cherished, not brushed aside like pesky flies.*

His actions and his words had endeared her to him. And that scared her. Especially since she found herself spending more and more time with him.

"Sorry I'm late." Hillary hurried up the walk wearing a pair of denim capris and a sleeveless white button-down shirt.

Clint went to meet her. "Thought maybe you'd chickened out."

The blonde's dark eyes narrowed. "Clint Stephens, since when have you ever known me to be a chicken?"

Lily leaned toward Carly. "They're more than just friends, aren't they?"

"Definitely. I'm just waiting for Clint to figure it out."

Lily couldn't help laughing. "Well, if there's one thing I've learned this week, it's that Hillary is quite a dynamo. Thanks to her, the rodeo school now has a top-notch website." She gestured to the vinyl banner on the side of the wagon.

"Hey, that looks great."

"We ordered it online, using the website header Hillary designed. And thanks to overnight shipping—"

"All right, gang." Clint waved everybody in. "Time for us to get in line."

"What about Lacie and Kenzie?" Carly glanced up and down the gravel street as a sheriff's vehicle pulled up. Lacie climbed out and made her way toward them while Matt released Kenzie from the back seat.

"Sorry about that." Dressed in navy shorts and a flowing red ruffled tank, Lacie eyed the little girl. "Someone had a hard time deciding what to wear this morning."

Carly smiled at the dark-haired girl in Matt's arms. "Sometimes those things just can't be rushed."

Noting the cuter-than-cute stars-and-stripes short ensemble, Lily added, "I think your outfit is perfect, Kenzie."

Matt set her to the ground. "You have fun, and I'll see you later today."

"Okay, Daddy." The five-year-old hugged him before turning her attention to Piper. "Want to sit by me on Grandpa's trailer?"

"Sure."

The two took off for the trailer, where Andrew and Daniel lifted them into the bed.

"Guess we'd better load up, too," said Carly.

"I'll be right there." Lily crossed the drive to where Colton waited, careful to keep a safe distance between herself and the horses. "Are you ready?"

"I'm more than ready." He nudged his cowboy hat back, the way Noah often did. "This is gonna be so cool."

After a year of nothing but negative attitude, she appreciated seeing her son so happy and eager to participate in something. "You do what Noah tells you to do out there, all right?"

"I will."

"He'll do fine," said Noah.

"Of course he will. He has a good teacher." Shielding her eyes from the midmorning sun, she looked up at Noah, her heart doing a weird flippy thing that had her quickly shifting her attention to Megan. "You look great, sweetie. Have fun out there."

Hurrying to join the others in the wagon, she felt heat creep into her cheeks. Unfortunately, it had nothing to do with the sun and everything to do with one ruggedly handsome cowboy.

By the time the parade began, though, Lily wasn't sure she'd ever felt more energized. Sitting in the back of the hay bale–lined farm wagon with Piper, Kenzie, Lacie, Daniel, Carly and Andrew, she peered out over Ouray and all the visitors and townsfolk that lined Main Street for the annual Fourth of July parade.

At the front of the wagon, Clint was all smiles, sitting atop the bench seat, reins in hand, steering them along the parade route. Hillary sat beside him, waving and tossing candy to the spectators. A true family affair.

As an only child, these were the kind of moments Lily used to dream of. And while she and her kids weren't part of the Stephens family, Clint and his sons had not only invited them in, they'd made them feel welcome. And she found herself wishing it didn't have to end.

Looking left and right, Lily tried to take it all in. The festive decorations, the aroma of smoking meat wafting from the Elks Lodge up the street and the sound of an airplane engine as a biplane zipped across the crystal clear sky, leaving a curlicue contrail and cheers in its wake.

This was going to be the best Fourth of July ever.

Later, after games at the park and lunch at Andrew and Carly's, they all returned to Main Street for the fire-hose water fights.

"Mom." Colton's green eyes were alight with something between joy and mischief. "Megan says we'll get really wet if we watch from the street." He pointed to the north and south end of the intersection where a barricade had been set up to block vehicles. "Can I?"

"I don't know." While she was certain the idea sounded enticing to her son, especially on such a hot day, she deferred to the other adults, particularly Carly. "What do you think?"

"Sure." Carly held a hand over her eyes to block the sun. "But stay together and keep in mind that there's a lot of pressure coming out of those hoses."

"Enough to knock both you kids over," added Noah. "So I wouldn't get too close."

"We won't," they responded in unison before running off.

"Famous last words." Noah chuckled, leaning closer. Close enough for Lily to smell the faint aroma of his soap. "I meant to ask you, how do you feel about your ex running for state senate?"

Lily practically spewed the water she'd just taken a sip of. "What?"

His brow puckered in confusion. "You mean you don't know? It was all over the news this morning."

She blinked. "I haven't turned on the news since we've been here."

"In that case, Wade Davis is running for state senate."

"Why?" She stared blankly, searching her mind for some clue as to what could have compelled Wade to do such a thing. He'd never had any political aspirations before.

I won't be able to take the kids this summer. My associates and I are working a deal that's going to require my undivided attention. Was that what he was talking about?

"He is in the oil industry," said Noah. "Perhaps he's got some ulterior motives."

"I can guarantee it." Because Wade Davis had motives for everything he did. And they were usually self-serving.

She thought about her children. Wade could have at least given her a heads-up so she could prepare them. Even though they weren't apt to run into any reporters here in

Ouray, they needed to be aware. And what if Wade wanted to take them on the campaign trail? Use them as pawns in his latest game?

No, she refused to dwell on it. She took another drink and recapped the bottle. "I know one thing for sure."

Noah's shoulder touched hers. "What's that?"

"He won't be getting my vote."

"I kinda figured that. And if I lived in his district, he wouldn't get mine, either." His easy smile had her heart racing.

Fortunately, the fire-hose fights began, and it wasn't long before she found herself thoroughly engrossed. Who knew such a thing existed? Teams of people aiming fire hoses at each other, trying to knock each other down. She loved each and every minute of it.

"What are we doing next?" Colton was soaked to the bone when he and Megan rejoined them.

Her brow lifted. "You mean *after* you change your clothes?" Fanning herself with a flyer someone had handed her, she watched Megan continue on to find Carly.

"Well, if I remember correctly—" Clint eased alongside Noah "—the activities are in a lull until the fireworks."

Colton smiled. "I have an idea then."

"Let's hear it." Lily waited.

"We could go horseback riding at the ranch."

Her breath caught in her throat.

"And this time you could go with us, Mom."

"Oh, I'd like that," injected Piper.

Lily's hand went to her neck. This wasn't supposed to happen. This was her day away from the ranch and horses.

Her stomach churned. *God, what am I going to do?*

Noah recognized the glassy look in Lily's eyes. Her tremulous smile. And if he didn't do something fast, she'd find herself in the midst of another full-blown panic attack, like that first day when she came to the stable with her kids.

Except they weren't at the stable. They were in the middle of Main Street, surrounded by hundreds of people.

What should he do, though? He couldn't keep enabling her. Granted, her fear was valid, but why was she so afraid to tell her kids? Sure, they were young, but they'd understand, wouldn't they?

He cupped a hand around Lily's elbow, hoping the touch might snap her back to her senses. "That's not a bad idea, Colton. I don't know, though. What do you think, Lily?"

Looking up at him, she swallowed, her expression nowhere near as carefree as it had been only moments ago. "I—"

"Colton!" Everyone but Lily turned at the sound of Megan's voice. And though it was Colton's name she called, she seemed to address all four of them. "Aunt Lacie invited me to go to the hot springs pool with her, Uncle Matt and Kenzie, and she said you and Piper could come, too."

Just the reprieve Lily needed. That was, if Colton went for it. The kid had fallen in love with horses, though, and had been talking about another family ride for some time.

Lacie approached then. "Just wanted to let you guys know that it was my and Matt's idea to invite the kids." She looked from Colton to Piper. "Have you two been to the hot springs pool yet?"

Piper squinted up at the Lacie. "I've been wanting to go, but Colton always wants to be at the ranch."

"Oh, I see." Tucking her long caramel-colored hair behind her ear, Noah's sister-in-law knelt beside the little girl. "Well, you're more than welcome to come with us even if your brother decides not to."

Piper's blue eyes went wide and shifted to her mother.

"Can I go, Mommy? Please, please, please." She prayed her hands together.

Slowly emerging from her stupor, Lily regarded her daughter first, then Lacie. "You—you're sure you don't mind?"

"Not at all. Kenzie loves playing with Piper."

Behind Lily, Dad rubbed his chin. "You know that place is going to be packed—"

Hillary shushed him with an elbow to the ribs then smiled. "My granddaughters love the hot springs pool. Especially now that they've added those new slides."

"They have water slides?" Colton's interest was suddenly piqued.

"You mean you haven't seen them?" Megan looked at Colton in eleven-year-old disbelief.

He shook his head.

"You really need to come with us then." She nodded very matter-of-factly.

Lacie glanced at the sun still high in the western sky, then her watch. "Matt gets off work in about thirty minutes. That should be just enough time for everyone to gather up their suits and towels and meet over at our place."

Smoothing a hand over her red-and-white-striped tank, Lily regarded Matt's wife. "That's very nice of you to do this. Thank you."

"Not a problem. It's not like we have to entertain the kids. Matt and I will just sit back and watch."

"Yeah, if you can get Matt off the slide." Not that Noah wouldn't do the same thing. Those things were fun no matter what your age. He turned his attention to Lily's son. "What do you say, Colton? Horses or hot springs?"

The kid scuffed a sneaker over the concrete sidewalk, trying to be nonchalant. All the while his eyes were alight with excitement. "I guess the hot springs would be kinda fun."

"Kinda, huh?" Noah ruffled the boy's wet hair. "Come on. Let's head over to your place so you two can gather your stuff."

After dropping the kids by Matt's a short time later, Noah and Lily strolled Ouray's side streets, savoring the quiet before heading to Andrew and Carly's for an evening barbecue and fireworks. Of course, the time alone also gave Noah an opportunity to address the elephant in the room.

"You almost had another panic attack when Colton brought up horseback riding."

Lily nodded but kept her focus on an ornate Victorian home.

"I get that you're afraid. But do you think it's fair of you to keep lying to Colton and Piper?"

The glare she sent him was filled with indignation. "I wouldn't lie to my children."

"Ever hear of lying by omission?"

Again, she studied the house. Not to mention the trees, fences...

They eased around a corner, the silence between them heavy, filled only by the sound of gravel crunching beneath their feet and the chirps of broad-tailed hummingbirds swarming a nearby feeder.

Yet for as much as he wanted to let it go, he couldn't. "You're not being straight with them, Lily. As far as those kids are concerned, you enjoy horses and riding every bit as much as they do."

Though her gaze remained fixed straight ahead, her features relaxed. "You think so?"

"I know so. Didn't you hear Colton? He didn't want to go riding today just to ride. He wanted to go riding with you. Something he didn't get to do the last time." Noah stopped then and turned her to face him. "You said you'd let me help you. And now that your foot's better, it's time for you to hold up your end of the deal." He hesitated, choosing his words carefully. "Either that, or you're going to have to tell Colton and Piper the truth."

She let go a sigh. "I know you're right. It's just…" She lifted a shoulder. "I can't tell my children I'm afraid. They look up to me. Count on me to be there for them, to take care of them. If I tell them I'm afraid of horses, they'll lose faith in me."

"No, they won't. Not if you tell them why you're afraid."

"But they'll think I—"

"Lied to them."

She lowered her head. "I guess you're right."

Touching a finger to her chin, he encouraged her to look at him. "I don't want to be right, Lily. I want to help you. But to do that, you have to be willing to step out of your comfort zone and accept that help."

"And therein lies the problem." She pulled away from his touch.

"What?"

"Leaving my comfort zone. It's so…comfortable."

He couldn't help chuckling. "Are you always this difficult?"

"No. I usually like trying new things."

"Such as?"

She shrugged. "Zip-lining, sushi—"

"Wait a minute." He held up a hand. "You'll eat raw fish that could have who knows what in it, but you're afraid to get on a horse?"

At least she had the decency to look embarrassed. "I know it sounds silly—"

"Oh, it sounds more than just silly."

She was quiet for a moment. Then, "What would be truly silly, though, is to tell my children the truth when I haven't even made the effort to overcome my fear." She looked him in the eye. "If you're still willing to help me, I'm ready to accept your help."

His smile was instantaneous. "Then I'll see you Monday morning."

Standing there in the shade of an aspen tree, he searched her pretty face, feeling his heart swell with something that hadn't been there in a long time. Respect? The thrill of a challenge? Or something else he was too afraid to name?

Chapter Ten

To say Lily was nervous when she pulled into the ranch Monday morning would be an understatement. Yet for all of her anxiety, she had one thing going for her. Determination.

Noah was right. She either needed to overcome her fear of horses or come clean with her children. Only problem was, now that she'd resolved to overcome her fears, what might Noah expect from her? Would he make her get on Duke again? Or perhaps some other horse?

She wasn't sure she was ready for that.

Small puffy clouds dotted an otherwise blue sky as she got out of her SUV.

"Mom, do you think maybe we could go to the hot springs tonight?" Colton emerged from the back seat. "Megan said they're open until, like, ten. We could go after dinner."

She chuckled, tossing her door closed. And to think Megan practically had to twist his arm to get him to go the first time.

"I think we can arrange that." After today, she'd probably be ready for a good soak.

"And I can show you all the cool stuff." Piper took hold of her hand as they started inside.

"Oh, I'd like that."

"Good, you're here." Clint was waiting for them just inside the entrance.

"We are, indeed."

"Noah was called away on an emergency, but he'll be back soon." His gaze bounced between her and the children. "In the meantime, he asked me to work with Piper on her riding while Jude helps Colton with his roping skills."

And what about her? Was she supposed to wait for Noah? Not that she minded. Anything that delayed her having to get on a horse was fine by her.

"Oh." Clint twisted her way. "And Noah suggested you help Megan feed and brush the horses."

Feed and brush? That would involve getting up close and personal with the horses. Touching them. Or worse, the horse might touch her. With its teeth.

She cleared her throat. "What kind of emergency did he have?"

"Equine rescue."

She wasn't sure what all that entailed, but having witnessed Noah's passion for horses, she was certain he was the right man for the job.

They were still in the lobby when Megan came around the corner. "Good morning."

"You're going to help my mom?" Colton seemed confused, if not disgusted, by the notion.

"No." Megan's response was very matter-of-fact. "She's going to help me."

"Why?" He looked from Megan to Lily.

Megan shrugged. "Because Uncle Noah said so." Turning toward Lily, she said, "Are you ready?"

"As ready as I'll ever be." She followed the girl, wondering if she had any idea just how true that statement really was.

After Megan armed Lily with two buckets of feed, they continued down one of the corridors lined with stalls.

"You like helping your uncle Noah?" She followed the girl.

"Uh-huh. It means I get to be around the horses."

Hmm... Too bad Lily couldn't say that. "You like them, huh?"

"Oh, yeah."

When they finally stopped, Lily read the wooden sign attached to the outside of the stall. "So this horse's name is Cookie?"

"Yes, ma'am." Megan slid the wooden and metal door to one side. "She's sweet, but she likes to eat a lot. Do you want to brush her or feed her?"

Neither, really. "I don't know. What do you think?"

The girl grabbed a long, oval brush that hung just outside the stall and handed it to Lily. "Just brush it across her back and sides. She'll like it."

"That's good to know." Because the last thing she wanted to do was make this horse mad.

She eyed the tan-colored animal for a moment. *God, please don't let this creature hurt me.*

With a bolstering breath, she set the brush on the horse's back and made a couple of short strokes.

The horse let go some kind of sound that had Lily taking a giant step back.

"Did I do something wrong?"

The girl smiled, shaking her head, sending her strawberry blond ponytail swaying back and forth. "No, that means she likes it."

Lily let go the breath she'd been holding. "Okay, good."

Resuming her position next to the horse, she started brushing again, this time using longer strokes.

"Miss Lily, could you help me with the feed bucket?"

"Of course, sweetie." Still holding the brush, she reached for the bucket with her free hand. That's when she felt it. Cookie was trying to bite her other hand.

She jerked it away, letting out a loud yelp as she dropped the bucket to the ground, toppling it, spilling the feed.

"She tried to bite me!" Lily's heart pounded against her chest.

Megan laughed. "She wasn't trying to bite you. She was looking for a treat."

Lily clasped her hand against her chest. "She what?"

The kid continued to giggle. "That's why her name is Cookie. She's always looking for a treat."

"Oh." Feeling more than a little foolish, Lily slumped against the wall. "Megan?" She tried to slow her breathing.

"Yes, ma'am?"

"I'm going to trust you to keep this little episode just between us. Because if Colton gets wind of this, I'll never hear the end of it."

Megan finally stopped laughing. "It's okay, Miss Lily. I promise not to tell."

"Thank you, sweetheart."

After sweeping up the spilled feed, the two continued on to the next horse. And though Lily did her best not to make a fool of herself again, she was no more comfortable than before.

They were on their way back to the feed room when they heard Clint yell for Jude. The urgency in his voice was unmistakable.

She turned to see Clint moving quickly down the corridor, toward the side of the building.

"What's going on?" she asked as he passed. "Is something wrong?"

"Noah's back."

Jude jogged past her then, bypassing his father and continuing toward the large garage door–style opening at the side where they moved the horses in and out of the building.

Still confused as to what all the hoopla was about, she gathered the kids and followed.

She leaned toward Megan. "Do you have any idea what's going on?"

"Uh-uh."

Outside, they stood in the shadow of the stable as Noah opened the back of a small horse trailer.

Peering inside, she was able to make out a lone horse.

Noah eased beside it. "It's all right, girl." His voice was gentle and filled with compassion. "Come on. I'm not going to let anybody hurt you."

Hurt her? What was that all about?

Several minutes passed and nobody moved. Not Clint, not Jude. Everyone, including the hands, just stood there at the side of the building, watching and waiting. Even the air was still.

Lily pulled Piper against her, uncertainty and curiosity plaguing her mind. What was going on?

When the horse finally emerged, Lily's heart nearly stopped.

The animal looked nothing at all like the powerful, intimidating creatures she was used to seeing. This horse was emaciated, its hair matted and baring what looked like open wounds. Its hooves were deformed.

"What happened to it?" Colton's gaze remained riveted to the horse.

"She's been neglected," said Noah. "From the looks of things, for a pretty good while."

"Poor horsey." Piper leaned into Lily, her bottom lip protruding.

"That's so sad," said Megan.

Noah eyed his father and brother. "We need to start her on antibiotics right away."

"I'll get things set up." Jude rushed past Lily and the kids on his way inside.

"Call the vet, too," Noah hollered after him.

Try as she might, Lily couldn't stop staring at the pathetic creature. Its dark eyes were almost…lifeless.

"Dad, help me get her inside." Noah held on to the horse. And no wonder. The poor thing struggled for each step.

Lily's stomach clenched at the sight. She might not be a fan of horses, but how someone could treat any of God's creatures this way was beyond her comprehension.

Noah continued to coax the horse. Patiently. Gently. The intensity in his eyes was like nothing Lily had ever seen before. "I've got you, girl. You're gonna be all right."

Had truer words ever been spoken? Because anything or anyone in Noah's care was in good hands. So why did she find that so difficult to accept?

Noah felt like a heel the next morning. He'd promised to help Lily yesterday. To at least begin to help her overcome her fear of horses. Instead, he'd spent all of Monday focused on this rescue horse. What else could he do, though? When these calls came, you had to do whatever needed to be done. If he'd ignored it, he'd have felt even worse.

Yet thoughts of Lily continued to plague him. The way she'd hung around all day had him wondering if she wasn't waiting for him to be done with the horse and start working with her. Perhaps feeling as though she'd taken second place. And to a horse, of all things.

Noah wasn't used to breaking his promises. But in this case, he hadn't had much of a choice. He hoped Lily understood that. She seemed to, but then, maybe she was simply being polite.

From his bed of hay in the corner of the horse's stall, he looked up at the pitiful creature. With so much going on—trail rides, lessons and prepping for the rodeo school—he really didn't need the addition of a rescue animal right now, but there was no way he could have turned it down, either. It's a wonder this poor girl was even standing.

If he lived to be a thousand, he'd never comprehend how people could be so cruel. Didn't they realize that animals had feelings, too?

Especially horses. When they were neglected or abused, their wounds went beyond the physical. And while the emotional scars might not be visible, they had the power to leave an animal unable to trust ever again.

Thoughts of Lily again played across his mind. She'd been betrayed by someone she'd trusted, too. And he'd witnessed just how difficult it was for her to take him at his word. At first, it had bothered him that she'd questioned his integrity. Now, though, he had a better understanding.

He leaned his back against the wooden wall, contemplating the horse. Earning this gal's trust would be the hardest part of his job. Because judging by the look in her eyes, she'd all but given up.

For the moment, though, he'd focus on her immediate physical needs and pray the mental recovery would follow.

Movement outside the stall brought him to his feet. He was surprised when it was Lily's face that appeared on the other side of the door. She'd had to walk past a lot of horses to get here.

She wrapped her long fingers around the bars. "How's she doing?"

Approaching the door, he noticed that Lily looked tired. Her green eyes weary. As though she hadn't slept well. Her long reddish-blond hair had been pulled into a ponytail that trailed down her back.

"The vet gave her some electrolytes, but I still haven't been able to get her to eat."

"That's not good, is it?"

"No. Even though she can only have a very small amount every few hours, her body badly needs the nourishment." Realizing Lily had to stand on her tiptoes to see, he reached for the door and slid it aside. "You can join me."

She did but never took her eyes off the horse. Nor did the horse take her eyes off Lily. Both appearing more cautious than afraid.

"Where are the kids?" He made more space for her.

"Your dad intercepted them. Asked them if they wanted to ride out with him on the UTV to check cattle."

"I imagine they were all over that."

Lily's laugh was soft. "Yes, they were."

He continued to watch her, seemingly unable to stop. "We didn't get a chance to talk yesterday. Did you help Megan with the horses?"

Still transfixed by the horse, she said, "I did."

"And?"

"No panic attacks, if that's what you're getting at." Hands tucked in the pockets of her jeans, she rocked back on the heels of her boots. "And only one momentary freak-out."

"What happened?"

The pink in her cheeks heightened when she finally met his gaze. "I…thought one of the horses was trying to bite me."

"Uh-oh." That would only add to her anxiety.

She scrunched her nose. "I may have made a little noise before Megan informed me she was simply looking for a treat."

"Ah." He relaxed then. "That would be Cookie."

"That's the one." Her focus returned to the horse. Like a mother watching a sick child. "Do you take in rescue animals very often?"

"Only when necessary." He swiped a sleeve across his brow. Having been here all night, he was coated in grit and probably didn't smell that great, either. "It's been a few years since we've had one."

"What's going to happen to her?" Removing her hands from her pockets, she started to reach toward the animal, then withdrew.

"Only time will tell. For now, we tend to her immediate health needs."

A horse nickered somewhere down the aisle, and another echoed in response.

"I feel sorry for her." Lily briefly glanced his way. "First to be treated so horribly, then to be taken to a strange place with people you don't know."

"It'll take time to earn her trust. She's been hurt, so trusting won't come easy."

"Looks like she and I have something in common." Again, Lily reached out a hand.

He took hold of it, directing her toward the animal's head. "Let her smell you. Then you can stroke her nose."

Fear flickered in Lily's eyes, but only for a moment. She took a step forward and did as he instructed.

He watched the silent exchange between horse and

woman. As though each recognized their own fears in the other.

"You're a good girl." Lily cooed, stroking the animal's muzzle. "But you need to eat, sweetheart. Otherwise you won't get well."

Her words surprised Noah. They didn't sound at all like someone who was afraid of horses. But of a mother talking to her child. And he had the strangest feeling the horse was responding.

Reaching behind him, he grabbed a small handful of alfalfa. "Lily?"

When she looked his way, he held out the feed.

"See if you can get her to eat this."

She stared at him for a long while.

He understood her hesitation. But if the horse would respond to her...

Slowly, she held out her free hand, allowing him to give her the feed.

Returning her attention to the horse, she again stroked its nose. "Shall we try eating a little something? Not too much, just a little." She brought her other hand to the animal's mouth. "I hear this is good stuff." Her voice was sweet. Almost childlike.

Noah was pleased when the horse sniffed the alfalfa. Encouraged when she didn't turn away. And he had to clamp his mouth shut to contain his excitement when the horse began to nibble.

Lily turned wide eyes his way, her smile one of amazement. "She's actually eating," she whispered.

"I know," he whispered back, reaching for another handful.

The horse ate that, too.

"You did it, Lily." He moved alongside her, wrapping an arm around her shoulders. "You got her to eat."

But Lily's focus was still on the horse. "Good girl." She ran a hand up the animal's nose. "Doesn't it feel good to get something in your tummy?"

After a few more minutes, she stepped away. "I'd like to help take care of her. If that's all right."

Speechless, he simply stared at the amazing woman before him. Not only was it all right, he had a feeling it would benefit her as much as the horse. And in the process, perhaps he could find a way to earn the trust of both.

Chapter Eleven

Lily wasn't sure why she wanted—perhaps even needed—to care for this horse, yet something had compelled her. Maybe it was the desire to prove something to herself. That she was stronger than her fears.

Of course, when she'd made that decision yesterday, her children weren't with her. Now?

"What's her name?"

Inside the stall, she looked from the malnourished rescue horse to her daughter, who was crouched in the corner, drawing hearts in the dirt floor with a piece of hay. "She doesn't have one yet." At least, she didn't think so. She'd only heard Noah refer to the animal as "the rescue."

"We should give her one then."

Lily scooped a small amount of food from the pail she'd left outside the door.

Somehow, the horse must have known what she was doing, recognized the sound or something, because when Lily turned around, those big, dark eyes were fixed on her. And though they weren't menacing or anything, it was still a little unnerving.

She swallowed hard as she moved slowly toward the horse and the plastic bucket attached to the wall.

Midway, the horse bumped her arm with its nose.

Lily felt her eyes widen as memories again flew to the forefront of her mind.

While some of the feed spilled onto the floor, the remainder went flying through the air when Lily jumped. At least she managed to silence her scream before it escaped.

Standing, Piper giggled, wrapping her arms around her middle and doubling over. "You looked funny, Mommy."

How embarrassing.

"She startled me, that's all." Lily glared at the animal that was now eating the feed off the floor. That's when it dawned on her. The horse wasn't trying to get to her— she simply wanted to eat.

Boy, did she feel like an idiot. "You're hungry, aren't you, girl?" She stroked the animal's head, knowing that was a good sign.

She promptly grabbed another small scoop, this time managing to get it into the feed bucket. And as the horse continued to eat, she couldn't help smiling. Who would have imagined that, with all of Noah's knowledge and love for horses, she'd be the one to get the animal to eat?

They'd spent the rest of yesterday going over how to care for the horse. Small feedings every few hours, water, tending her wounds and plenty of TLC.

Strange, for as much as she disliked horses, she found the loving part the easiest. Probably because this animal needed so much of it.

"Mommy?"

"I'm sorry, Piper. What is it?"

"We need to give the horse a name."

She took a step back, tugging her daughter with her, giving the animal space. "Okay, what do you think we should name her?"

"We could give her a princess name, like the twin

horsies Megan showed me. She named them Elsa and Anna."

"I see." Lily wondered how the guys felt about that. "In that case, two princess names are probably enough." Leaning against the wooden wall, she continued to watch as the rescue finished the food and moved to the water. *Good girl.*

Turning to face her daughter, she said, "Do you have any other suggestions?"

The girl's face contorted. "Let me think."

"All right. And while you do that, I'm going to check this horse's wounds." When she'd first seen the animal, she'd thought it was covered in sores. Yet once Noah gave her a good washing with some medicated soap, Lily realized that most of what she'd thought were wounds was actually dirt.

Approaching the horse, she began to second-guess herself. Maybe she should wait and do this when her daughter wasn't here to watch her. She'd already made a fool of herself once. She'd hate to do it again.

Smoothing a hand down the animal's side, she winced at the defined outline of each and every rib. *This is so wrong.*

"You know, Piper, when this gal stepped out of that trailer yesterday, I never would have guessed she had such a pretty honey-colored coat. Would you?"

Her daughter gasped. "That's it, Mommy."

She must have missed something. "What's it?"

"Her name." Piper moved closer with no fear whatsoever. "Honey."

Lily looked from Piper to the horse. The color of the hair, the animal's seemingly sweet disposition... "I think it's perfect. We'll have to run it past Noah, though."

"Run what past me?" He appeared in the doorway of the stall, his cowboy hat tilted back, his work shirt dusty.

"Honey." Piper beamed and practically bounced out the word.

He looked confused. "You're going to run past me with honey?"

The girl giggled. "No, silly. The horse. Her name should be Honey."

"Oh." He eyed the animal a moment. "It fits." He again looked at her daughter. "Honey it is then. Good job, Piper." He held out his fist.

The girl bumped it with her own. "Mommy helped, too."

"Well, in that case—" He turned his attention to Lily. "Good job, Mom."

"Mommy?" For whatever reason, her daughter was suddenly wearing a pouty face.

"What is it, sweetie?"

"I'm hungry."

She wasn't surprised, given that the child had barely touched her eggs this morning.

"Well, guess what, kiddo?"

Tilting her head, Piper looked up at Noah, curious.

"Miss Hillary just brought us a big ol' pan of cinnamon rolls from Granny's Kitchen."

Her daughter's blue eyes flickered back to life as she licked her lips. "I like cinnamon rolls."

"Why don't you run on up to the office and get one then." He watched as she darted out of the stall. "And make sure my dad doesn't eat them all."

"Wash your hands first," Lily called after her. When she turned back around, she observed how much more rested Noah appeared this morning. "You sure made her day."

"I do what I can." He eyed the horse. "How's it going in here?"

Shoving her hands into the back pockets of her faded jeans, she decided not to tell him about the little mishap with the feed. "Good, I think. She seemed quite eager to get her food."

"I'm glad to hear that. Have you checked her wounds?"

"No, I was just about to."

"Good. Why don't you go ahead and do that while I'm here?"

Great, another opportunity to potentially embarrass herself.

"Oh, and I talked to the farrier." He retrieved the equine first-aid kit from the wall just outside the stall. "He's going to try to get out here this afternoon or tomorrow to start working on her—on Honey's hooves."

She glanced down at the animal's misshapen feet. "That is kind of gross."

"I know." He opened the plastic box. "It's also not good for the horse." Pulling out some gauze pads and a tube of ointment, he handed them to her. "I'm ready when you are."

Hmm...how much time do you have?

Taking the items into her hand, she drew in a bolstering breath and moved to Honey's hindquarter.

"Any sign of blood?"

"A little, maybe." She stood on her tiptoes for a closer look.

"Wipe it with the gauze. Any blood will show up there."

She loosened a couple of squares from the stack, pressed them against Honey's hair and started to wipe the wound. The horse's skin twitched beneath her fingers.

Honey jerked her head in Lily's direction.

"Oh, my!" Her hands shot into the air. She dropped everything and pressed her back against the wall, her heart beating like a bass drum against her ribs. "What just happened?"

Noah reached for Honey's halter, shaking his head. "That was my fault."

"Your fault?"

"Sorry about that. I should have held on to her so she couldn't jerk like that."

"Why did she jerk?" Lily cautiously bent to pick up the gauze and ointment.

"Your kids ever fuss when you're doctoring a scrape or cut?"

"Yes." She rose slowly, her hands shaky.

"Same thing. Honey here was simply reacting."

Lily shook her head, trying to understand. "So, you knew she was going to do that?"

"Suspected, yes." His matter-of-fact response grated her already frazzled nerves.

"You suspected she might do something yet you not only didn't hold her, you failed to warn me?" Her breathing intensified.

He scratched his head then, looking rather sheepish. "When you put it like that…"

"How could you do that to me?" She took two steps in his direction, her gaze narrowed. "You know better than anyone how terrified I am of horses."

"I said I was sorry."

"Well, sorry doesn't cut it, buster." She poked a finger into his chest. "I trusted you and you—"

He took hold of her wrist and stared down at her, an annoying grin tugging at his lips.

"Let me go." Her nostrils flared as she glared up at him.

"You trust me?" He smiled in earnest now.

"*Trusted.* Past tense." She yanked her hand free, tossed the items at him and continued out the stall door before looking back. "I won't make that mistake again."

Noah watched Lily storm up the corridor with determined steps that quickly ate up the distance.

She'd trusted him? And he'd let her down.

He quickly closed the stall door and took off after her. Somehow, he had to make this right.

You should have held on to that halter.

"Lily!"

She didn't even slow down. Instead, she made a left at the arena, probably headed for the door then her vehicle and back to town.

He picked up pace, dirt pounding beneath each booted step. He'd just reached the arena when Jordan Stokes, one of his hands, met him.

"Hey, boss."

"Not now, Jordan." He continued past the lanky college-aged kid.

"Williams hasn't shown up, and his student is waiting."

Reluctantly, Noah slowed as Lily ducked into the front office. Probably to grab Piper.

He turned slightly. "Has anyone heard from him?"

"He called Amber to say he had a flat tire. We're just wondering what to do with his student in the meantime."

"Can you cover until he gets here?"

The kid shook his head. "I've got some folks saddled up and waiting to go out on the trail."

Noah heard the door open then. He twisted to see Lily and her daughter disappear behind it.

"Tell the student I'll be right there. I have to take care of something first."

"Sure thing, boss."

Noah jogged toward the door and threw it open. Just in time to see Lily driving away.

His heart sank. Any other time he would have gotten in his truck and gone after her, but unfortunately, that wasn't an option now. He let the door close and started back toward the arena.

The riding lesson was almost over when his absentee instructor finally arrived, meeting him in the arena.

"Sorry about that, boss." The remorse in Seth Williams' eyes was hard to miss.

Noah gave him a nod. "It's all right, Seth. Life happens." And although the timing of his flat tire couldn't have come at a worse moment, it wasn't the kid he was upset with, just the circumstances.

He eyed the student, then his employee. "I'll let you take over." With that, he left them and headed back to check on Honey. Best he could hope for now was to catch Lily when she came to pick up Colton from work later. And then pray she'd at least hear Noah out.

Approaching the stall, he noticed the door sitting open. Strange, he thought for sure he'd closed it. He peered through the bars.

"I'm sorry I ran out on you like that." Lily stood inside the stall, gently stroking the horse's muzzle.

He took a step backward, his mind racing. She'd come back. When? And why hadn't he seen her?

He leaned forward just enough to continue to watch.

"After all, I said I'd take care of you." She looked into the animal's eyes. "Of course, you probably didn't think I was doing a very good job when I hurt you. I wasn't trying to. But sometimes we have to endure a little pain before we can heal."

Pulling back again, he wondered what he should say. He could apologize profusely or act like nothing ever happened. Or settle somewhere in the middle. Though he wasn't quite sure where that was.

Whatever he decided, at least Lily was here.

He took a deep breath and continued into the stall, as though he didn't know she'd returned. As if the sweet lilac aroma of her perfume wouldn't have tipped him off.

She turned at the sound of his footsteps. "Noah." She didn't appear to be upset anymore. Though she didn't seem to want to look him in the eye, either.

"You're back."

Her nod was subtle as she stepped away from the horse, wrapping her arms around her middle as she moved toward the back of the stall.

He followed her. "Lily, I'm sorry for what happened earlier. I don't know why I didn't hold on to Honey's halter. All I know is that I didn't, and for that I am truly sorry. I never meant for you to be frightened."

She still refused to look at him. She just kept nodding, staring at the dirt-covered floor. How was he supposed to interpret that?

After a long silence, her green eyes finally met his. "I accept your apology. But I owe you one, too."

Okay, now he was confused. "For...?"

"Overreacting."

"I'm not so sure about that. I mean, given what happened to you when you were younger, it's understandable."

"That doesn't give me the right to blame you. I mean, what if you hadn't been here? She—" Lily gestured toward the animal "—would have reacted the same way."

"True. But as you pointed out earlier, I could have warned you."

Falling quiet again, she leaned against the wooden wall. "I'm madder at myself than anything." She lifted her gaze. "I really do want to help this horse. After what she's been through, I have no doubt that she's every bit as afraid and distrusting of humans as I am of horses. So in reality, her reaction to me treating her wound was the same thing as me startling when she reared her head back."

"I hadn't thought of it that way..."

Pushing away from the wall, she moved to Honey's side and ran a hand over the horse's neck. "I don't want her to be afraid of me. So from now on, at least where Honey's concerned, I'm going to have to check my fear at the door."

"You want me to put a bucket out there?" He pointed outside the stall, a grin tugging at the corners of his mouth. "For your fear. Wheelbarrow, maybe? Eighteen-wheeler?"

"Stop." She smiled then. Exactly what he'd hoped to achieve.

Joining her beside the horse, he said, "You know I'll do whatever I can to help you."

"I appreciate that." She sucked in a breath. "For now, though, I think Honey and I need to get to know each other a little more. Start building that trust."

"I think that's a good idea." And as he absently rubbed the horse, he found himself wondering if he shouldn't do the same. Get to know Lily more and start rebuilding that trust.

Chapter Twelve

Lily had never been so eager for a worship service to end.
Though it had nothing to do with the pastor's sermon and
everything to do with the oppressive heat that seemed to
have overtaken Ouray the last two days.

Since most places in the town were not air-conditioned,
including Restoration Fellowship, they relied on ceiling
fans, open windows and the cross flow of air to keep
things cool. But the air coming through those windows
today felt more like a furnace.

Standing in the shade of the large fir tree in front of
the church, Lily fanned herself with this morning's bulletin while she waited for the kids. They had yet to join
her because they were too busy enjoying their conversation with Clint. She had to find a way to escape this heat.
At least until sundown.

Maybe there was movie theater nearby.

No, that would be too much like their life in Denver.
She wanted something out of the ordinary. Something
they couldn't do in the city.

She fanned harder. There was always the hot springs.
Not that she or any one of the hundreds of other people
there would want to indulge in the actual hot portions of

the pool. Perhaps they should consider the reservoir over in Ridgway. That was bound to be cooler. And on a day like today, probably every bit as crowded as the pool.

Maybe a trek into the mountains. Someplace nice and secluded, just her and the kids, where she wouldn't be distracted by a certain good-looking cowboy.

She let go a sigh. No matter what she decided, she'd still need to stop and check on Honey. She was pleased with the way the rescue horse was coming along. Something she supposed she could say about herself, too.

Never had she been more ashamed than when she walked out of the stable on Wednesday. Yet, since then, things had been different. She'd been different. She felt stronger, more confident. As though she might really be able to overcome her fear.

The small congregation continued to file out of the sweltering building until she finally spotted Colton and Piper with Clint. Seeing the three of them together, the enormous smiles on their faces, always warmed her heart.

The patriarch of the Stephens family was like the grandfather her children never had. With her parents and Wade's father gone and his mother's aversion to children, Lily often felt bad that Colton and Piper weren't able to experience that special grandparent-grandchild bond like the one she'd had with her grandma Yates.

When Lily was growing up, there were times when she'd spent more time with her than her own parents. Her grandmother was the one who'd told her about Jesus and how He died for her sins. She'd taught Lily to cook, to crochet and even how to do laundry. Something Lily's mother never would have done because, as far as she was concerned, laundry was the maid's job.

Lily shook her head. Lois Yates had had money, too, yet she knew and appreciated the value of a dollar. Having grown up poor, she always said, *Why would I waste perfectly good money paying someone for something I can do myself?*

Only one of the reasons she'd loved her grandmother so much. She was in high school when the woman passed away, and she still remembered feeling as though she'd lost her best friend.

Watching her children now, she suspected that their bond with Clint was something they'd miss when they returned to Denver. Perhaps even more than the horses.

Just then she saw Noah leave the building with Jude and Daniel. All three of them were grinning from ear to ear. The trio sneaked up behind their father and the kids before Noah continued toward her.

"We have an idea," said Noah.

The smiles on their faces had her lifting a brow. Because whatever they were contemplating had them pretty excited. "What's that?"

He waited as the kids drew closer. "What would you guys think about spending the afternoon by the river out at the ranch?" His gaze bounced between Colton and Piper. "My brothers and I could show you how we used to cool off when we were kids."

"You mean, like, swim in the river?" Colton's eyes were wide, his face red from the heat.

"More like splash and play, but yes."

Lily paused her fanning and leaned toward him. "That river water moves pretty fast. Are you sure it's safe?"

"Absolutely. The snowpack is gone, so things have calmed considerably since that day we were there. Besides, we're not going to be in the main part of the river."

She eyed a couple with a toddler as they passed. "Then...where will we be?"

"There's a little fork that breaks off at the bend. It's

deep enough to sit in, cool off and play around, but without the current."

"When we were younger—" Jude gestured toward Noah and Daniel "—and the weather was like this, we practically lived there."

Noah turned his head slightly so only she could hear him. "The water's still mighty cold, though."

"Ah. Thanks for the warning," she whispered.

Addressing the group again, Noah continued, "If that sounds like something you'd be interested in, we could make a day of it. Build a fire to roast some hot dogs, maybe make some s'mores later…"

"I'm in," said Colton.

"Me, too." Piper bounced up and down.

"Don't forget about me." Clint raised his hand.

"Where's Hillary?" Lily was used to seeing her and Clint together.

"She's working today, but I'll see if she can join us later."

Everyone looked at Lily then.

Cooling off in the river on a sweltering day like this did sound enticing. So why did it bother her so much? Given all the time she'd been spending at the ranch, one would think she'd be used to it by now.

Perhaps that was the problem. She was getting *too* used to being around a certain cowboy. Making her heart long for things that, until recently, she'd considered off-limits. Things like a second chance at love. Which was foolish, given that she and her children had to be back in Denver in a month. Because wherever her kids were, she'd be there, too.

Unfortunately, Noah's idea was the best she'd heard all day. And since she was planning to go check on Honey, anyway…

She tucked the bulletin inside her Bible. "You had me at s'mores."

"Good." Noah rubbed his hands together. "Why don't you and the kids go change and grab whatever you think you might need, and we'll meet at the ranch."

"Okay, but do you think we could take Honey with us? You know, give her a chance to get some fresh air and exercise. That is, unless you don't think she's up to the walk or that the heat would be too much for her."

"No, I think that's a great idea. There's plenty of shade where we'll be. And now that the farrier's seen to her hooves, yeah, we can give it a try."

"Good. I think she'll appreciate the change of scenery." And so would Lily. But she'd best keep her mind on her children and Honey. Otherwise, there was no telling where her heart might lead her.

Seeing Colton and Piper's flushed faces in church this morning, Noah knew he had to do something to help make the heat more tolerable for all of them. Once he mentioned it to Jude and Daniel, it didn't take long to come up with a solution.

Now as he stood in the shade of a large cottonwood tree, clad in swim trunks, listening to the sound of children's laughter, he knew he'd made the right decision. For them as well as him. And he hoped to make this day memorable for all of them.

He couldn't remember the last time he'd spent a day on the river, just having fun. But being out here today, playing and goofing around with his brothers and Lily's kids had him feeling like a younger man, instead of a forty-year-old ex–rodeo champ. Perhaps it was the freezing-cold water that had renewed him. Or the pretty blonde feeding Honey a few feet away.

He shook his head in disbelief. Lily might not know much about horses, but she knew how to love. And that rescue horse needed love.

In only five days under Lily's care, Honey was eating regularly. Her eyes flashed with life, and she was always on the lookout for Lily.

But the biggest change of all was that Lily actually seemed comfortable around the horse. Even in the stable. And whether it was working with Honey or sheer determination that had brought about the transformation, Lily and the horse had formed a special bond. Understanding each other in a way no one else could.

He sucked in a breath as a blast of freezing-cold water hammered into his back. Turning, he spotted a grinning, swimsuit-clad Piper holding one of the water soakers he'd grabbed from the house. A move he was now regretting.

Retrieving another soaker from the bucket, he followed her into the water. "Oh, so you think that's funny, huh?"

Even as he dipped the tip into the water and pulled back the plunger to fill it, she continued to laugh.

"Let's see how you like it." Afraid of hurting her, he took aim at her legs and fired.

She squealed and tried to run away, but to no avail. The water hit his target.

Without missing a beat, the little stinker shot right back at him, this time hitting him smack-dab in the middle of the forehead.

He dropped his soaker and clutched his pretend wound before stumbling to the bank and collapsing on the ground. He stayed there, unmoving, until he heard footsteps approaching. Small footsteps.

With a roar, he sat up, scooped the little girl into his arms and tickled her.

She wriggled. "Stop." And giggled. "Stop."

He quit then, allowing both of them to catch their breath. Yet, as he watched the water drip from her two blond ponytails, he wondered if this was what it was like to be a father. The joy, the playfulness, making memories... How he wished he'd had the opportunity to find out.

Colton approached then. "Can we go exploring?"

"Sure." He set Piper on the ground and stood. "We used to do that all the time."

"Cool." The kid eyed his mother. "Hey, Mom?"

She stroked the horse one last time before heading their way. "What's up?"

"Want to go exploring with us?"

Shoving her hands into the pockets of her denim shorts, she said, "Sounds like fun."

Dad, Jude and Daniel emerged from the water, and Noah suddenly felt as though he'd gone back in time.

"You guys want to come with us?"

Jude shook his head. "Wish I could, but I need to get ready for work."

"And I need to run up to the office to check on some equipment." Daniel draped a towel around his neck. "I'm taking a group for an all-day rafting trip on the Gunnison River tomorrow."

"That sounds exciting." Lily looked more than a little fascinated.

Noah's baby brother was the adventurer in the family. He traveled all over the world white-water rafting, snowboarding and who knew what else. For some reason, though, he'd decided to stay home this summer. And Noah kind of enjoyed having him around again.

"It can be." Daniel looked from Lily to her children. "You should check out our tours sometime."

She smiled. "I just might have to do that."

"I reckon I'll head on out with these two." Dad waggled

a thumb between his two youngest sons. "We'll leave you all one of the utility vehicles so you can haul everything back to the house." His gaze moved to Lily. "Mind if I take Honey back with me? One less thing you'll have to worry about later."

"No, not at all. Thank you, Clint. And I'm sorry Hillary couldn't make it today."

The older man waved a hand. "Aw, I'll see her soon enough."

"Well, tell her I said hello."

"Will do." He waved as he started toward the horse.

Lily looked at Noah and her children and shrugged. "Guess it's just us then."

Noah threw on a T-shirt and flip-flops as Colton took the lead while his sister did her best to keep up.

They were almost to a wooded area when Colton stooped and started picking at the ground with his fingers.

"Whatcha got there, Colton?" Noah moved closer. "A rock?"

"I think it's an arrowhead." The boy continued to dig.

"Man, I used to search high and low for those when I was your age. My father always told me there weren't any, but—"

"I got it." The boy stood. "It is an arrowhead." He held it out to Noah.

He took hold of the triangular, rough-cut piece of rock and let go a chuckle. "It sure is. Humph. Just wait till the old man sees this."

"Can I keep it?"

"Of course you can." He handed it back to Colton, thoughts of fatherhood again plaguing his brain. Making him wish for things that would never be. He cleared his throat. "It'll be your souvenir of our day on the river."

He shook off the emotion as the four of them continued into the woods. A breeze rustled the leaves on the trees as birds sang sweetly overhead, flitting from branch to branch.

"You know what I like most about Ouray?" Lily glanced his way, the ground crackling beneath her canvas shoes.

"The charming cowboys?" He grinned, hoping to lighten his mood.

Her brow lifted. "Close, but no."

"I give up then." He eyed the children as they ran ahead.

"Ouray makes me feel...normal. As though I'm okay just the way I am."

Hands stuffed in the pockets of his trunks, he said, "I guess I'm not following you."

"My entire life, all I've ever wanted is to have people accept me for me. Not for what I have or what I could do for them. Not Lily the real estate mogul's daughter or Wade Davis's wife, but just me. And aside from my grandma Yates, just me has never been good enough. Not for my mother, not for my husband." She paused. "Have you ever been in a room full of people and still felt alone?"

That he could relate to. "Just about every time I went into the arena."

Her smile was one of understanding.

"What's that place?"

He glanced up to see Piper pointing. Only then did he realize they were at the cabin. His cabin. His home. The place he'd avoided for the past twelve years.

Why hadn't he paid better attention to where they were headed?

Because you were enjoying yourself.

"What a cute cabin." Lily approached the neglected log home. "That lilac bush smells amazing."

He recalled the day he and Jaycee had planted it. It was one of her must-haves for the house because she loved the smell of lilacs. Now it had overtaken the entire north end of her beloved home.

Lily stepped onto the porch as though taking in every detail. "Was this somebody's home or, maybe, a hunting lodge?"

"Noah said it was his house." Colton looked from his mother to Noah.

"Can we go inside?" asked Piper.

His mind swirled at the thought. All the memories he'd locked inside, not wanting to ever see them again.

His insides twisted and turned. He began to sweat even though he felt cold.

How could he say no without sounding like a jerk? "I, uh, I don't have a key."

Liar. You know there's one hidden behind the outlet cover.

Obviously sensing his unease, Lily urged her children off the porch. "That's okay, kids. Perhaps Noah can show us another time."

There would be no other time. Of that, he was certain.

Yet, rather than telling them why, he'd lied. *What kind of guy does that just because he doesn't want to do something?*

A coward, that's who. Someone who had no respect for others or placed no value on trust. Someone like Wade Davis.

Well, Noah was no coward.

Forgive me, Lord.

"Wait." He held up a hand to stop them. "There's a key behind the outlet cover by the door if you'd like to let yourselves inside. If you don't mind, though, I'll stay out here."

"That's all right." Lily came alongside him, understanding in the green depths of her eyes. "We don't need to see it."

He thought about the beautiful river-rock fireplace and hand-carved beams. Building this house had been a labor of love, and he'd enjoyed every minute of it.

Pride sparked inside him once again.

He glanced at Lily, smiling. "I built it myself."

She looked from him to the house. "Now I'm intrigued."

"Three bedrooms, two baths." Suddenly curious as to what she might think of it, he nodded in the direction of the cabin. "Go ahead and have a look. I'll be here when you're finished."

Her gaze searched his for the longest time. Finally, "We won't be long."

"This is so cool."

Noah couldn't help chuckling when he heard Colton's echo from inside, even if it was his usual comment whenever something impressed him.

A short time later, Lily closed the door and returned to his side. "You are a man of many talents, Noah Stephens. The craftsmanship in there is beyond anything I've seen before. It's truly beautiful." Her words wiped away his anxiety.

"Thank you." Looking down into her green eyes so filled with life and love, he couldn't help thinking about what she'd shared with him as they walked. "Earlier you said that just Lily has never been enough. Well, I've spent a good bit of this summer with who I believe is just Lily, and you know what I think?"

"What?"

"Not only is she enough, I think Lily's perfect just the way she is."

Chapter Thirteen

Lily stood in front of the washing machine the next morning, staring at the rain streaking down the window. How could today be so gloomy when yesterday had been perfect in every way?

She eyed the small pile of swimsuits and shorts. Okay, maybe not every way. But, thanks to Noah, they'd sure made the most of what would have otherwise been an unbearable day.

One by one, she tossed the clothes into the washer, recalling the look on Noah's face when they were at the cabin. Like a scared little boy who'd been left all alone. It was then that she realized that it wasn't just any cabin. It was the home he'd shared with his wife. And given all of the photos she'd seen when she went inside, the memories that still lived there were too much for him to bear.

Reaching the bottom of her laundry pile, she spotted the jacket Noah had wrapped around a chilled Piper last night, after the sun set. She picked it up, brought it to her nose and inhaled. It smelled of fresh air, horse and masculinity. Just like Noah.

How sweet it had been to see him so playful with her daughter. But the sight of him holding a sleepy Piper as they sat around their little campfire, roasting marshmallows, was what really got to her.

I think Lily's perfect just the way she is.

His words played through her mind for about the fiftieth time this morning. And once again, she found herself wondering what it would be like to have the love of a man like Noah. Someone who appreciated her for who she was, instead of trying to turn her into someone else. Someone strong and caring who adored her children and actually wanted to spend time with them.

A clap of thunder brought her to her senses. She tossed the jacket into the washer, closed the lid and pressed Start, mentally kicking herself. Even if Noah was over his wife, which he obviously wasn't, what was the point? They'd be heading back to Denver in a month. And Noah was no more likely to come there than she was to stay here.

It was time for her to get the kids up to head to the ranch, anyway. Aside from their lessons and seeing after Honey, she'd received emails from two magazines, *Cowboy News* and *Rodeo Magazine*, wanting to schedule interviews with Noah. Meaning she had no choice but to talk with him about timing before she responded.

Yet, when they arrived at the stable, Noah was eager to get going with the kids' lessons, which was fine by her. Her thoughts from earlier this morning had her feeling rather embarrassed. Not that he knew any of them, but still…

While Piper's instructor worked with her, Lily made her way down to see Honey. She'd checked on her before heading back into town last night, concerned that the day's heat might have been too much for her, but she didn't appear any worse for the wear. If anything, she seemed happier. Perhaps because she'd had the opportunity to get out of the stable and enjoy the outdoors for a while.

Looking left, then right, she observed the other horses

as she passed their stalls. Some watched her, while others were oblivious. Mr. Withers always nodded when she walked past, and Dakota did this weird thing with his mouth, as though he was smiling real big.

She stopped in her tracks.

She was actually looking at the horses. Not keeping her eyes to the ground as she would have a week ago. She was learning their names, their habits.

Leaping into the air, she did a fist pump. "Yes!"

Suddenly aware that she might not be alone, she slowly scanned the area, relieved when she saw no signs of anyone.

She continued down the aisle, listening to the varying intensity of rain on the metal roof. She found the sound rather soothing, so long as the rain didn't fall too hard. Then it was just plain loud.

"Good morning, my Honey girl." She slid the door aside. "How are you doing today?"

The horse nickered her own greeting as Lily stepped inside.

"Did you sleep well?" She stroked Honey's muzzle. "You were probably worn out from that long walk yesterday, weren't you?"

The horse flicked her ears.

"And now you're hungry." Over the past week they'd gradually increased the amount of food Honey received, as well as the length of time between feedings, and it seemed to be paying off. The animal was actually showing signs of plumping up, though she still had a long way to go.

After Honey was squared away, Lily returned to the arena, eager to talk with Noah about the interviews. His first one had been very well received, at least judging by the number of inquiries they'd received via the website. Something that had her thinking.

Once the rodeo school was up and running, perhaps Noah should consider some sort of a summer camp. That way he'd be able to bring in students from across the nation as opposed to the region.

Seeing that lessons were still going strong, she continued on to the front office. Maybe Clint was there.

Instead, the place was empty. Not to mention messy.

She moved to the desk, noting the empty clipboards. Of course, with the rain, there were no trail rides this morning. Still, Noah should have someone to take care of these little things, freeing him up for all the other stuff he did. Like running a business.

Locating the consent forms, she attached them to each of the clipboards, hung them on the wall in the lobby and then organized the desk. At least that would make things a little more efficient.

"I wondered where you were."

She turned as Noah walked into the office.

"Did you do this?" He pointed to the desk.

She lifted a shoulder. "I needed something to pass the time."

"Lily, you have no idea how much I appreciate that. Sometimes I feel like I'm on my own here."

Uneasy with his praise, she said, "I need to talk to you about something."

"Okay. And then I have something for you."

Something *for* her?

She briefly explained about the magazine interviews. "For now, they'll be for their online versions. However, it could lead to an entire spread in an upcoming issue."

"I like the sound of that." He paused. "At least, I think so."

"It's a good opportunity."

They looked at the calendar and came up with a handful of dates she could offer the magazines.

"Oh, and before I forget." She grabbed her tote bag from the chair, pulled out his jacket and handed it to him. "I washed it, so you're good to go."

"Thanks." He set it aside and took hold of her elbow. "Now come with me."

She couldn't help noticing the way he grinned as they walked in the direction of the arena.

"Where are the kids?"

"Piper's helping Colton put Sonic up, and then I told them they could get a snack from the storage room."

"That ought to keep them busy for a little bit."

He nodded, opening the gate to the arena. "You've been doing very well with Honey this week, and I've observed that you're much more relaxed, even when there are other horses around."

She stepped inside, recalling her little happy dance a short time ago. "I've noticed that, too."

With the sound of rain on the roof filling the momentary silence, he led her across the arena to where a lone horse still remained. "I was thinking, perhaps, we might try building on that." He stopped beside the horse.

She eyed the animal, then Noah. "What do you have in mind?"

"I thought maybe you could try a short ride."

Her heart skipped a beat, but she quickly recovered. "I don't think I'm up to that just yet."

"Okay." Seemingly confused, he shifted from one booted foot to the next. Tilted his cowboy hat back. "Then what if you tried sitting in the saddle for a few minutes?"

She swallowed hard. Helping Honey was one thing. She wasn't as robust as this horse. What if this one didn't like her?

Stop this nonsense, Lily. You're overreacting. Her mother's words taunted her.

"Come on, Lily, give it a try." Smiling, Noah patted the animal. "Checkers is a good horse. Mild mannered."

Her gaze drifted past him, searching for her children. They were nowhere in sight.

She looked at the horse. Her pulse raced. She knew she needed to do this eventually. And that she'd come a long way. But— *You're acting foolish, Lily.*

Was she? Like when the horse bit her and she cried? Had she been foolish when that same horse sent her crashing to the ground, breaking her arm? Even Noah had understood her fears.

"Lily…" He leaned closer, his smile teasing. "Come on. Don't you trust me?"

Her gaze darted to his. Why did he have to say that? She did trust him. But what about the horse? What if it didn't like her? Or sensed her fear? She'd heard Noah say countless times how good horses were at sensing a person's feelings. If she got on this horse with apprehension and fear pulsing through her veins, there was no telling what could happen.

So tell him.

And have him think her a fool, too?

She watched him for several moments, silently begging him to understand. When he didn't, she shook her head. "I'm sorry, I just can't."

Then, with disappointment blurring her vision, she hurried away.

All of this rain was getting depressing.

Oh, who was Noah kidding? His moodiness had nothing to do with the weather. Lily didn't trust him. And the knowledge of that, coupled with gray skies and daily rains, had made this one miserable week.

Trail rides were down to mornings only and, with the ground growing more saturated by the day, things weren't looking good. If the rain kept coming—which was likely, given southwestern Colorado's annual monsoon season— things would soon be too slick to risk taking the horses up the mountain.

Sitting at his desk, he thumbed through a stack of invoices and packing slips for items that had been delivered for the new arena. But for the life of him, he couldn't locate the one for the chutes he'd ordered. They were supposed to have been delivered last week, yet he had no record.

He reached for his cup of coffee, knocking it over. With a loud growl, he sprang from his chair, sending it rolling across the floor. He quickly snatched all of the paperwork out of the way before grabbing a rag to sop up his mess.

Seemed he was good at making messes lately.

He tossed the rag aside. Why wouldn't Lily trust him?

Because you messed up, remember?

When he forgot to hold Honey's halter. But he thought they'd worked that out. Evidently he'd thought wrong. He'd barely seen Lily this past week. Sure, she still brought the kids and cared for Honey, but she'd virtually ignored him. And that hurt.

Pacing, he jammed his fingers through his hair. How long had he known Lily now? Four, five weeks? He should not be hurting. They were barely more than acquaintances.

Actually, she knows more about you than most people.

That was his fault for not keeping his mouth shut. Something that only served to further frustrate him. Lily was leaving in a few weeks, and his heart belonged to Jaycee.

He could not keep dwelling on this. He had a business to run. Meaning he needed to find out where those chutes were.

Turning, he marched out of the office and headed next door to the new arena. Perhaps Andrew, who was also his contactor, would know something.

"Andrew!" he hollered as he entered the large metal structure. The word echoed throughout the empty building.

"Over here."

The sound of power tools filled the space as he strode toward the far end of the building, ready for something to finally go his way.

"What's up, bro?" Andrew lowered his hammer.

"There were some chutes that were supposed to be delivered last week, but I can't seem to find any paperwork on them. Have you seen them?"

"Chutes aren't coming until next week."

"What do you mean? I scheduled them for last week so I'd have time to inspect them before they were installed."

"Sorry 'bout that." He swiped a sleeve across his brow. "I changed it to next week for fear they'd be in the way."

Noah's blood pressure ratcheted. "Who are *you* to go changing my deliveries?"

"*I'm* the one who has to find a place to store these things so they're not in our way." He motioned a hand across the space. "We're still building here, you know."

"Yes, I know. You're building for me."

Andrew sighed. "Look, I'm sorry I didn't check with you before I changed the delivery date. Next time I'll be sure to do that."

"Next time?" His voice echoed again. "There'd better not be a next time, brother."

Andrew pulled back. "What's got you so stressed out?"

"I can't imag—"

"Noah?"

Andrew nodded, indicating he should turn around.

When he did, he saw Lily standing a few feet away. Dressed in jeans, a gray Ouray T-shirt and rubber boots, she appeared timid. And though it killed him to admit it, his insides tangled at the sight of her.

"Is everything all right in here?"

Noah and Andrew exchanged a look before Noah said, "Yeah. Everything's fine."

She clasped her hands in front of her. "Well, they didn't sound fine." She glanced left then right before taking a step closer. "I could hear you next door."

Sure, he was mad, but had he really been that loud?

"Noah, I need your help with something. Honey's having a problem."

He cut his brother a parting glance.

Noah and Lily had entered the stable a few moments later when she said, "I finally heard back from the magazines I told you about regarding the interviews."

He'd all but forgotten about that. "And?" Following Lily around the corner, he caught a whiff of her lilac perfume.

"*Rodeo Magazine* will be here next Thursday, and the other will be the following Monday."

He fought to gather his thoughts. "That should give me time to regroup between interviews." He paused outside Honey's stall. "So what's the problem?"

"Um…" She poked her head inside the stall. "Honey's out of food."

He simply stared. "Did you really need me for that?"

"No, it was just an excuse to get you away from Andrew."

Suddenly realizing how irrationally he'd been behaving, he chuckled. He'd been taking his frustrations out on his brother, much like when they were younger. "I guess I was acting rather juvenile."

"Um, yeah. So what's the real problem?"

"Real problem?"

"Yes. Something's obviously bothering you. Because the man I saw in there was not the Noah I know."

He crossed his arms over his chest. "Then maybe you don't really know me."

Shifting, she said, "Maybe. But I don't think that's the case."

A silent moment ticked by, the two of them in an apparent battle of wills.

Looking away, he leaned against the opposite stall. "You must have been busy this week. Haven't seen you around here much."

Now she refused to make eye contact. "I guess I was hiding." She opened the stall door.

"Hiding?"

She looked at him then. "I walked away from you last week without any kind of explanation. Leaving you with the impression that I don't trust you."

Did that mean— Straightening, he moved closer, eager to know. "Do you? Trust me, that is?"

"I do."

The tension in his shoulders eased.

"It was the horse I didn't trust." She continued, "But at the time I was too afraid to tell you."

"I don't get it. If you trust me, why were you afraid?"

She shrugged. "I don't know." Her gaze lowered momentarily then bounced back to his. "No, that's not true. I do know."

He waited for her to continue.

She squared her shoulders. "All my life people have

discounted my feelings. 'Lily, don't be silly. Lily, you're overreacting.' I got good at keeping things to myself."

Relief and sadness mingled as he reached for her hand. "Lily, I don't ever want you to be anything but real with me."

Her nod was quick. Too quick. She turned away and tried to break free, as though she didn't believe him.

But he refused to let go. He wanted her to understand that he wasn't like those other people.

Still holding her hand, he waited for her to look at him.

When she finally did, he smiled and said, "Just Lily is my friend, and I like her just the way she is."

Chapter Fourteen

Sitting at the desk in Noah's office late Wednesday morning, Lily stared at the Ouray visitor's guide, longing to see more of the San Juan Mountains. Since the first time her friend Kayla had mentioned that Ouray was the jeeping capital of the world, she'd been intrigued. The thought of traveling old mine roads built almost a century and a half ago and seeing a landscape that had been virtually untouched by man had sparked her desire to spend the entire summer here. And yet there was still so much she hadn't seen.

Then again, when she planned this trip, horseback riding had never entered her mind, let alone roping lessons, riding lessons, promoting a rodeo school and caring for a neglected horse. Not that she was complaining. Because even though her plans might have changed, there was plenty of good coming from those changes.

Still, if she could find the time…

"Mommy, look." Her daughter gestured to the stack of clipboards now complete with consent forms.

"Thank you, Piper." She closed the booklet and set it aside. "You did a very good job." Lily had been trying to help out in the office more.

"What's going on?" Noah strode into the office just then, with Colton not far behind.

"Just taking care of some paperwork for you." She pushed away from the desk and stood. "How was the trail ride?" The rain had stopped Monday afternoon, leaving plenty of sunshine and pleasant temperatures in its wake.

"Good. Soggy in a few low spots, but we were able to make it onto the mountain."

"Yeah and we saw some bear tracks." Colton's green eyes were wide. Since there were only three people in the group, Noah had invited him to go along.

"But no bears," Noah was quick to add before addressing her again. "What have you two been up to?"

"Not much." She picked up a piece of paper from the desk. "Travis Vasquez's mother called to say he won't be able to make his lesson today or anytime in the near future." She held out the paper, meeting Noah's gaze. "Apparently he has mononucleosis."

"Mono? The kissing disease?"

"Eww." Piper's face contorted as she petted Patches the cat.

Lily chuckled. "I...think I've heard it called that."

"You mean you can get a disease from kissing?" Colton looked from her to Noah and back, and she wasn't sure if she should be alarmed by his interest or not.

"That's right, Colton." Noah sent her a stealthy wink. "So you'd better watch out." Grinning, he continued, "Looks like I'll be able to work with both of you kids this afternoon then."

Lily bit her lip, her gaze drifting to the sunlight pouring through the window. "How's the weather looking? Any clouds?"

"Nah, they're saying it's supposed to be another nice afternoon."

"Hmm…" She eyed the visitor's guide, wondering if all the tours for this afternoon were already full. If not, maybe they could get in. Otherwise, she could drive down to—

"Did you ever take the kids to Ironton?"

She looked up, realizing that he'd caught her daydreaming. "No, I haven't found the time. However, if you wouldn't mind—" she mustered her best smile "—I was thinking I might see if we could get on a Jeep tour for this afternoon."

"A Jeep tour?" Colton whined. "What about my lesson?"

Noah grinned. "I've got a better idea."

Seemed no matter what she suggested, he always had a better idea. And while he had yet to let her down—

"What if I took you all to a place that's off the beaten path?"

Curiosity lifted her brow. "What do you call off the beaten path?"

"Someplace the tours don't go."

She liked the sound of that. "Go on."

"You like wildflowers?"

"I *love* wildflowers."

"I imagine with all this sun—" he motioned toward the window "—they're quite brilliant."

"Flowers?" Her son appeared more than a little chagrined.

Noah glanced his way. "Did I mention a couple of really cool glacial lakes, too?"

"Ooh, can we go swimming?" Piper beamed.

"Okay, so how do we get to this place?" Lily crossed her arms over her chest. "Rent a Jeep? Unless your truck can make it?"

"Truck's too wide. And our chances of finding an available rental Jeep are slim to none with this weather." He wasn't building a very good case.

"So what are we supposed to do?"

"Not to worry." He pulled his phone from his shirt pocket. "I'll simply call Matt to see if he'll swap vehicles with me for the afternoon."

Lily was afraid to get her hopes up. Yet a little over an hour later, they had grabbed a round of hamburgers at Granny's Kitchen and picked up the Jeep and were on a dirt road weaving their way into the mountains.

Since they'd removed the vehicle's top, the sun shone down on them, warming Lily's skin as well as her heart. This was even better than she'd imagined, and she could hardly wait to see where Noah was taking them.

Through sunglasses, she eyed the cowboy-turned-tour-guide in the driver's seat. With his Broncos ball cap, aviator sunglasses and stubble lining his jaw, he looked even more rugged than usual. Throw in the muscles straining the sleeves of his T-shirt, and any woman would swoon.

However, she'd seen the kind, wounded heart that beat inside Noah. The one that longed to help hurting people as well as hurting horses. The one that still grieved the loss of his wife. And that made it more and more difficult for her to resist him.

But resist she must. For her children, if not herself. Because August 15 would be here before they knew it, and then it would be back to life as usual, which sounded rather unappealing at the moment.

The engine groaned as the road grew steeper, and Noah came to a stop.

"Is there a problem?" Because this narrow road would be a really bad place to break down.

He adjusted the manual gearshift. "No, just switching over to four-wheel drive."

She let go a sigh. "That's good."

"Don't worry, Lily." His smile was reassuring. "You won't be disappointed."

They continued on, winding around a wall of dark gray rock that stretched toward the blue sky, while on the opposite side, a knee-shaking drop-off led to a valley blanketed with white-barked aspens and deep green conifers.

Colton poked his head between the two front seats. "Did they really used to bring mules down this road?"

"They sure did." Noah eyed the boy in his rearview mirror, both hands firmly on the steering wheel. "Back then it was the only way to get supplies to the mines and to bring the ore down, so they had to build these roads."

"They built them?" Colton peered down at the road. "How?"

"Dynamite."

"Whoa…"

Did Noah know how to capture the boy's interest or what?

"Yep, they dynamited out large chunks of the mountainsides all over this area, allowing them to create these roads we still travel today."

"Now that's cool." The kid leaned back in his seat, smiling.

"If you get an opportunity," Noah hollered over the engine, "you all should stop by the museum in town sometime. They've got a mine display in the basement where you can see and learn all sorts of stuff."

They moved on up the road, waving to other vehicles as they passed. Something that was very precarious in a few of the narrower sections and made Lily more than grateful that it wasn't her doing the driving.

When they finally turned off the main road, the first thing she saw was a relatively wide stream in their path. Fortunately, there was also a bridge.

Noah revved the engine, eyeing the stream. "Think we can make it, gang?"

"Yay!" cheered the kids.

Lily jerked her head toward him. "You're not seriously considering going through that, are you?"

"It's part of the experience."

"But what if we get caught in the current?"

"You're right. I'd better get a running start." With that, he put the vehicle into Reverse then, before she knew what was happening, they were moving headlong into the water.

She shrieked when the cold water splashed against her skin and couldn't help laughing at the sight of her children doing the same.

"That was cold," giggled Piper when they came to a stop on the other side.

"Yeah, but it was fun," said Colton.

"Things are going to get a little bumpier now." Noah eased on the gas. "So you might want to hold on."

He wasn't kidding, either. Moving into the woods, it felt as though they were bumping from one boulder to the next, making it impossible for her to take any pictures of the wildflowers lining the trail.

The air smelled of fragrant firs and earth as they picked their way up another rocky rise, then crept back down, only to repeat it one more time. Mud went flying and the back end of the Jeep came down hard, jolting them to an abrupt stop.

Everyone went silent. The only sound was that of the engine and some birds chattering nearby.

Noah adjust the gearshift. Eased off the clutch. Yet they didn't move.

He tried again, but to no avail. The tires continued to spin.

Hopping out, he rounded the vehicle, his brows drawn together.

Not a good sign.

Finally, he stood in front of them, hands perched on his denim-clad hips. "Sorry, guys, but it looks like we're stuck."

"Stuck?" Surely he was kidding.

"Stuck," he confirmed.

Her shoulders sagged. Now what were they supposed to do? It wasn't like roadside assistance could make it up here to help.

Disappointment wove its way through her. What about their destination? The wildflowers, glacial lakes and her off the beaten path?

Instead, they were stuck.

There was no way Noah was going to let Lily down. He'd promised to take her someplace special, and that's exactly what he intended to do. After all, this wasn't his first trip into the mountains.

Eyeing his passengers, he said, "Don't worry. We'll be on the road in no time."

"How?" Lily unhooked her seat belt and stood on her seat, batting a tree limb out of the way. "Are you going to push us out?"

Smiling, he took in the space around them, the position of the wheels. "While I appreciate your faith in me, that would not be a viable option. Fortunately, we have a winch." He moved toward the vehicle.

Lily was beside him in no time. "At the risk of sounding like a city girl, what's a winch?"

"That thing right there." He pointed to the spool attached to the front of his brother's vehicle, with a cable coiled around it.

She looked at it then back at him. "What does it do?"

"Gets us out of the mud." Reaching toward the contraption, he released the clutch. "Colton, would you grab that yellow strap from the back of the Jeep and bring it to me, please?"

"Yes, sir." The kid hopped out of the vehicle.

"Piper, would you mind keeping your mama company over there for me?" He pointed to a nearby rise.

"Okay." She unhooked her seat belt and jumped down.

"Good girl."

"Is this the one?" Colton came toward him, holding up the strap.

"That's it."

In no time, he and Colton had a length of cable pulled out and hooked to the strap Noah had looped around a tree several feet away.

"All right, gang. Looks like we're ready to roll."

With Lily and the kids standing a safe distance away, Noah attached the controller and turned the power on.

"Would you look at that," he heard Lily say. "That thing is pulling the Jeep right out."

"Cool," said Colton.

"Yay for Noah." Piper jumped up and down as the vehicle came to rest on solid ground.

He couldn't help chuckling. Having them around did wonders for his ego.

He turned off the power and faced his audience. "Anyone ready to see some lakes?"

They hurried back and piled into the vehicle while he disconnected everything.

When he returned to the driver's seat, he looked at Lily. "The journey is always better when there's a little adventure involved."

"Well, it was definitely a learning experience." She

hooked her seat belt. "And I'm sorry I doubted you. But now I'm ready to see some wildflowers."

"All right then." He shifted into gear, making a mental note to approach this section with a little more caution on their way out.

A short time later, they emerged from a forest of conifers into an alpine meadow covered with wildflowers in every color of the rainbow. Yellows, pinks, purples, reds and blues.

Lily's gasp was like a tickle on his ear. "Stop, please."

He readily complied as she stood on her seat, camera at the ready.

"This is incredible." She glanced down at him. "I've never seen wildflowers like this. So brilliant. So abundant." Her camera clicked multiple times.

Peering up at her, he said, "Can I move on up to the lake?"

She immediately dropped back into her seat, her smile almost childlike. "Yes, please."

She looked so cute. Like a kid with a long-awaited gift.

They continued through the meadow, its delicate floral fragrance wafting around them.

"Whoa…" Standing, Colton clutched the roll bar as they approached the lake. "How did the water get so blue?"

"Pretty cool, huh?" Noah brought the Jeep to a stop and turned off the engine. "It has to do with something called glacial, or rock, flour. It's so light that it stays suspended in the water. The sunlight reflects off it, giving the lake that unmistakable turquoise hue."

Lily's feet were on the ground in an instant. "I've lived in Colorado all of my adult life, and I've never seen anything as beautiful as this place." She twisted left then right, snapping pictures.

"That's because you've never been to Ouray." He lifted

Piper out of the vehicle as Colton jumped out the other side, then set her on the ground and watched her take off after her mother and brother.

Drawing in a deep breath, he took in the unmatched beauty of his surroundings. He hadn't been up here in years. Silver Basin was more brilliant than he remembered. The flowers, the lake…all of it above the timberline and hidden by craggy gray peaks. Here, his worries seemed to fade away.

Under a gorgeous blue sky, he looked around, surprised to discover they were the only people there. Something that could change at any moment, so they'd best take advantage of it.

"Come on." Approaching the water, he motioned for Lily and her children to follow him. "Let's walk around the lake." A task easily achieved since the upper lake wasn't that big. And the lower lake was even smaller. He'd show them that one on their way down.

"How come nobody's here?" Lily walked beside him as the children ran on ahead through vibrant green grass and over chunks of gray rock that had broken free of the mountains to dot the landscape.

He shrugged. "Like I said, off the beaten path. Not that it's always this way."

Her smile was beyond contented as she tried to take in every aspect of the area. "If I lived here, I think I'd come up here as often as I could, just to get away."

"Funny, my mother used to say the same thing."

"Did she come up here a lot?"

"As often as she could." He dodged around a large rock. "Which, I'm sure, wasn't near as often as she would have liked. This was her favorite place to escape."

"Your mom had good taste." Lily paused in front of a spruce to take some pictures of Colton and Piper tossing rocks along the water's edge. "Though with five boys, I can't imagine what she'd want to escape from." Lowering her camera, she sent him a knowing look that made him smile.

They began walking again.

"What was she like?"

Lily's question was unexpected. Yet, he knew it was because she cared. And it had been a long time since someone cared about him.

For a moment, he gazed at the sky, trying to gather his thoughts. "She was devoted to her family. Loved Jesus and horses. Was an amazing cook." He glanced toward Lily. "And I never saw a better example of a marriage partnership than the one between my dad and her. The ranch had been their dream from the time they first started dating in high school."

"Aww…" She paused to take another picture.

"They both grew up in town, but Dad loved old Westerns and Mama loved horses. So they started with one small tract of land when they got married and then added to it over the years."

"It must have been hard for your father when she passed away."

"It was hard for all of us, but yeah, he struggled." He shoved his hands into the pockets of his jeans. "Poured himself into the ranch, either to help keep her legacy going or simply to occupy his mind."

Lily looked up at him, tucking her long hair behind her ear. "How did she die?"

"Cancer." Unable to look at her, he stared up at the jagged peaks, blinking.

"It's obvious how much she meant to all of you."

"She was an amazing woman, all right. Had to be to put up with my father and us boys."

Lily puffed out a soft chuckle as they found themselves near the Jeep again.

"She knew how to keep all of us in line, including my father." He spied the kids running into the meadow. "Only one of the reasons we adored her so much."

Lily blinked several times. "What was her favorite wildflower?"

"Columbine, of course." Reaching down, he plucked one. "Though she was partial to anything purple or blue." He handed the flower to Lily. "You remind me of my mother in some ways."

She tilted her head. "I'm guessing the part about loving horses isn't one of them."

He felt himself grin. "No. But your commitment to your children, your determination to bring them up with morals and values, your faith… The two of you would have been fast friends."

She studied the flower in her hand. "That may be one of the nicest compliments anyone has ever paid me."

Staring down at her, his pulse quickened as emotions he hadn't felt in a long time wove their way around his heart. Emotions he hadn't felt since Jaycee died. Emotions he'd vowed to never feel again.

He took a step back.

"Hey, Mom!" Colton's voice had her turning around. "You gotta come see all these flowers."

Smiling, she said, "Well, now there's something I never thought I'd hear him say." She took off in the direction of her children.

He watched the three of them; his stomach twisting in knots as one thing became as clear as the water in these lakes.

Bringing Lily up here was a bad idea.

Chapter Fifteen

Lily stared out of the office window, grateful to Noah for taking them to Silver Basin. In part because her children had yet to stop talking about it. That and the fact that the rain had returned the next day, harder than it had been before. This time, the showers weren't relegated to only the afternoons. Instead, it had rained all day and all night for the past five days. Add that to what they'd received the week before, and everything was drenched, meaning no trail rides, no Jeep tours...

No wonder Noah had been so moody.

At least they were getting a small reprieve this morning, allowing her children to play outside for a while. For some reason, they found stomping around in the mud in their rubber boots fun.

Since Noah and Clint had gone off to help someone at a neighboring ranch, Lily had the office to herself, giving her the perfect opportunity to address the freshly printed VIP invitations for the open-house event. They now had demonstrations planned for the event—roping, barrel racing, bronc riding—as well as photo ops with Noah, cake, balloons...

She licked another envelope. If only she could talk him into getting a mechanical bull.

Reaching for another invitation, she prayed she and the kids would be able to make it back out here for the event. Labor Day was a long weekend, after all.

"Mom!"

"Mommy!"

The calls came simultaneously.

She pushed away from the desk and hurried into the lobby before her children decided to track mud everywhere. "What is it?"

Colton huffed and puffed as though he'd been running. "There's a calf in the pasture, and he's all by himself."

"He's crying." Piper pouted.

Slipping out of her shoes and into her own rubber boots, she said, "Let's go have a look."

She followed them out the door and up the drive, dodging puddles as she went until they reached the barn. Sure enough, in the middle of the muddy pasture, a cute little black calf stood unmoving, repeatedly calling for his mother.

Hands on her hips, Lily scanned the area, but she didn't see any cows.

"We have to save him, Mommy."

"Save him from what, Piper? Maybe his mama left him there on purpose and told him to stay put until she got back."

"But what if she forgot about him?"

Lily bit back a chuckle. "His mama won't forget. So I suggest we wait until Noah and his father get back and let them handle it."

Her children looked at each other, seemingly satisfied with her response.

"Can we keep playing?" asked Colton.

"Yes, you may. But try not to get too muddy, all right?"

"We won't."

Ha! She headed back to the stable. Like that was going to happen.

The phone was ringing when she stepped inside. She hastily stomped her boots on the mat before rushing into the office to answer it.

"Abundant Blessings Ranch."

"Yes, this is Lauren Pearson with the *Grand Junction Daily Sentinel*. I'd like to speak with Noah Stephens."

The *Grand Junction Daily Sentinel* was one of the newspapers she'd sent a press release to. "I'm sorry, he's not available at the moment. This is his publicist, Lily Davis. Is there anything I can help you with?"

"We're looking at doing a brief article on the rodeo school. Would you be able to answer a few questions?"

She wheeled the chair closer to the desk and sat down. "I'll do my best."

While the questions were easy enough, they dragged on forever. Glancing at the clock on the wall, Lily realized twenty minutes had passed and she hadn't heard so much as a peep from her children. They were either having fun or getting into trouble. Maybe both.

"Ms. Pearson, I thank you for your interest—"

"Mommy!" Piper cried as she swung the door open. "Help!"

"I'm sorry, I need to go." Lily hung up the phone as her daughter hurried into the office, tears streaming down her face.

"Colton fell into the river!"

"What?" She felt the color leave her face as images of her son being carried away by the current filled her mind.

Piper grabbed her hand and tugged her toward the

door. "Hurry, Mommy. He slid down the bank, and he can't get out."

With all the rain, the river was rushing fast and furious.

She had to get to Colton now.

"Come on." She pushed through the door and aimed straight for the UTV parked on the side of the building. "Hop in, Piper." She threw herself into the driver's seat and reached for the ignition. "Where's the key?" Her gaze darted around the vehicle. She hastily checked the glove box. Nothing.

"We could ride Duke?"

"Piper, I don't know how to saddle a horse."

"He's in the arena. Noah left him there."

Lily did not want to ride Duke. But she couldn't afford to waste any more time, either. She had to find her son.

"All right. Let's go."

Lily sprinted ahead, led Duke out of the arena and brought him outside before lifting Piper into the saddle.

She stroked the animal's muzzle. "Noah trusts you, so I guess I'm going to have to, too, Duke. Help me get to Colton."

With a deep breath, she put her foot into the stirrup, climbed into the saddle behind her daughter and urged Duke in the direction of the river.

The horse moved swiftly, his muscular legs eating up the distance faster than she expected.

Why had she let the kids play outside alone? She should have been watching them. She squeezed her eyes shut. *God, please let Colton be all right. Keep him safe. Don't let the water take him under.*

Approaching the river, the roar of the current heightened her anxiety. She pulled back on the reins. "Where is he, Piper?"

"Over there." She pointed. "By the tree."

Lily guided Duke to the tree then dismounted, dragging Piper with her. "Colton?"

"Here!"

Her gaze combed the muddy riverbank until she spotted him clinging to a tree limb. She rushed to where he was and dropped to her belly, the sodden earth soaking her shirt and jeans as she tried to reach him.

He was too far down. She tried to push her body out farther, tried to grab him, but it was too far. She'd risk going down, too.

"Hurry!" her son cried.

God, help me. I don't know what to do.

"Mommy?"

Turning, she saw her daughter pointing to the coiled rope attached to Duke's saddle.

"Hold on, Colton. I'll be right back." Lily leaped to her feet, sprinted toward the horse and grabbed the rope. She tied one end to the tree and then stretched it so she could send the looped end down to Colton. But the rope was too short.

She looked around, her breathing ragged. There was nothing close enough.

Her gaze drifted to Duke. The animal was massive. If he could hold Noah, surely he could support the weight of her son.

Knowing that was her only hope, she quickly untied the rope from the tree and returned to the horse, eyeing the saddle horn. She'd seen Noah, Colton and the other cowboys do this at least a hundred times. *Think, Lily.*

She had to climb into the saddle to reach the thing. When she did, she twisted the open end of the rope around the horn a few times, then cinched it under the last loop, praying it would hold.

Dismounting, she led the horse closer to where her son

held on for his life and lowered the looped end toward Colton. "Can you hold on to the branch with one hand long enough to grab the rope with your other?"

He glanced down at the rushing water, then back to her. "I—I think so."

She could see the fear in his eyes. He'd already been there so long. He must be exhausted, his muscles spent. *God, please don't let my boy fall. Give him strength.*

Her grip tightened on the rope as she waited for him to take hold. All the while never taking her eyes off her son. "You can do this, Colton. I know you can."

He nodded and, in one swift motion, let go of the branch and stuck his free hand through the loop before wrapping his fingers around the rope.

"Good job." The rope was taut. The length perfect. "Now the other hand."

Again, he nodded and, after a moment, he moved his left hand from the branch to the rope.

"Okay, good. Now hold on while I pull you up." But the more she tugged, the more her feet slipped beneath her. *God, help me!*

She straightened, the horse coming into her periphery. "Keep holding on, Colton," she yelled over the sound of the river.

A handful of steps and she was beside Duke. "Piper, stay back." She thrust herself into the saddle, took hold of the reins and pulled with all her might.

The horse took one step back. Then another and another.

"It's working!" Just like the Jeep up on the mountain. "Hold on, Colton!"

A few moments later, he appeared over the edge of the bank, his knuckles white as he continued to cling to the rope.

Lily's heart pounded. "Attaboy, Duke. Just a few more steps." She continued backward until her boy was on solid ground, then jumped down and rushed to his side.

She drew him into her arms as he tossed the rope aside. "Thank God you're okay." Setting him away from her, she smoothed a hand over his wet hair, surveying him to make sure he wasn't hurt. That's when she saw the tears streaming down his mud-streaked cheeks. "Oh, it's okay, baby." She clutched him to her again, her own tears falling as his arms wound around her waist. "You're safe. I've got you."

"I'm sorry, Mom. I know I shouldn't have come down here."

"No, you shouldn't have." She kissed his forehead. "But we can discuss that later. For now, let's get you back to the stable."

Clouds had filled the sky at some point during the ordeal, and the rain started to fall again as the kids climbed atop Duke. Lily took hold of the reins to walk the horse.

"What are you doing, Mom?" Her son was covered in mud. "You can get up here, too."

"There's not enough room in the saddle."

"That's okay. You can sit in the saddle with Piper, and I'll sit back here." He patted the spot just behind the saddle.

She knew Duke could handle the weight, but, "We can do that? I mean, he won't try to buck you off or anything?"

Her boy smiled then. A smile she'd never been happier to see. "No. We're not going that far, anyway."

"All right then." She climbed behind her daughter and felt Colton's arms around her waist. Relief washed over her along with the rain. By the grace of God, she'd done it. She'd saved her son. God had given her the strength and the wherewithal to do what she needed to do, including getting on a horse. She found she actually didn't mind it too much, especially now that Colton was safe.

Perhaps riding was within her realm of possibility, after all.

Noah watched the wipers on his father's pickup slap back and forth across the windshield, the gray skies a perfect match for his mood. "Just what we need. More rain."

Dad clutched the steering wheel. "Not like it's unexpected this time of year."

A sports car whizzed past them then, going well over the speed limit. And on a wet road, no less.

His father growled. "Everybody's in a hurry."

That's precisely why they'd spent the last few hours at Jim Osborn's ranch. Some idiot flying down the highway last night lost control and took out a good hundred feet of fence. Every rancher knows that cattle on the highway spells bad news for everyone, so Noah and his father had packed up early and gone to help put up a temporary barrier in order to avoid such a problem.

Now they were headed back to Abundant Blessings, where he'd no doubt have to face Lily again. After all, she had agreed to hold down the fort while they were gone. Still, since their trip up to Silver Basin, he'd been trying to keep things a little more businesslike between them. Call it self-preservation. But he'd made a vow. One he intended to keep.

Perhaps he could knock the kids' lessons out early, giving them no reason to hang around. Not that they ever really needed a reason. They'd simply become a part of everyday life at the ranch, and, as much as he didn't want to, he liked having them there. All of them.

He supposed he could make himself scarce by working in the new building. Now that the chutes and pens had been installed, his vision was starting to come to life. He'd be able to find plenty to keep himself busy and away from Lily.

Dad turned into the ranch, the truck rumbling over the cattle guard. "Want me to drop you at the stable?"

"Nah. I need to grab a fresh shirt."

They were almost to the house when his father leaned closer to the windshield. "Is that what I think it is?"

Noah looked up. "It can't be." He blinked once. Twice. "Lily's on a horse?"

"Not just any horse. That's Duke."

Noah puffed out a disbelieving laugh. "You have got to be kidding me." He smiled, wondering what could have convinced her to do that. In the rain, no less.

Yet there they were. Lily, Colton and Piper all riding Duke.

"I gotta find out what's going on." He piled out of the dually before it had come to a complete stop and jogged through the mud until he met them just beyond the house.

Lily smiled down at him, her long hair wet, her shirt and jeans covered in mud...and he felt something shift inside.

He continued to stare up at them, despite the rain pelting his face. "What are you doing?"

"Oh, you know." Lily lifted a shoulder. "It's such a beautiful day, thought we'd take a ride."

Well, his day had indeed gotten brighter. "No, seriously."

"Colton fell into the river." Piper was nothing if not candid. "But Mommy saved him."

Noah's chin dropped.

Lily nodded her confirmation while Colton appeared rather sheepish.

"What's goin' on?" Dad joined them.

"Colton fell into the river."

"Do you have to keep saying that, Piper?" Her brother frowned.

She twisted to look at him. "I'm just telling the truth."

Noah bit back a laugh. "Why don't we get out of the rain and you can tell us the whole story."

"Good idea," said Lily.

They heard a calf bawl.

"Aww, look, Mommy." Piper pointed across the pasture. "He's still there."

"Hmm... Doesn't look like he's moved." Lily looked left and right. "No sign of his mama yet, either." Her gaze lowered to Noah and his father. "The little guy's been crying all morning." She eyed the calf again. "Do you think he could be stuck in the mud?"

"It's possible." Dad studied the situation. "Guess I'd better go see if I can help the little fella."

"Can I come?" Colton straightened.

"Sure." Dad waved the boy down. "You're already muddy."

Colton swung his leg over, then paused. "Is it okay, Mom?"

She grinned. "Go ahead."

"I want to come, too." Piper started to get down, but her mother stopped her with a hand to her shoulder.

"It's all right," said Dad. "She can come."

Noah helped the girl down and watched her run off through the mud before returning his attention to her mother. "How about you? You want to help, too?"

"I think I'm good." She stroked Duke's neck. "But I am curious about what they're going to do."

"Dad'll just pick the calf up. Move him someplace safe, then wait for his mama to come for him."

"What if she can't find him?" Spoken like a true mother.

"She'll find him." He took a step back. "You comfortable riding Duke back to the stable or you want me to take over?"

"I think I'm good."

Actually, he was surprised just how relaxed she seemed to be.

She urged Duke forward, and Noah walked alongside them. "By the way, where do you keep the keys to the UTV?"

"In my pocket." He tugged them out to show her.

Looking down at him, she lifted a brow. "A lot of good they did me there."

"So what happened?"

All the way to the stable and on to Duke's stall, she explained what had transpired.

"You should have called me." He removed the horse's saddle and moved just outside the door to set it atop its stand.

"There was no time." She paced a few feet away, no doubt reliving everything in her mind. "All I could think of was that I had to get to Colton. Fortunately, everything turned out all right."

When she looked at him, he saw the angst in her pretty green eyes. Only then did he realize what she must have gone through. How terrified she must have been.

And he hated that he hadn't been here to help her. He clenched his fists, longing to take her into his arms and comfort her. To be that one person she could lean on.

But he couldn't.

He shoved his hands in his pockets and took a step back, dirt grinding beneath his boot. "You overcame your fear and got on a horse to do it."

Her smile grew wide. "I did."

"How was it?"

She studied Duke for a moment. "Not nearly as frightening as I thought it would be."

"I think you were already frightened."

"You'll get no argument from me there." Rubbing her arms, she turned away. "I've never been so scared. And not knowing what the situation was…" Her voice cracked. "It felt like everything was moving in slow motion. I was so afraid I wouldn't make it. That he'd—" She let go a sob. Her shoulders shook, robbing him of whatever resolve he might have had.

Closing the short distance between them, he moved in front of her and took her into his arms. "Let it out, Lily. It's okay, I've got you."

Her body melted against his as she continued to cry. "I was so afraid." She hiccuped.

"I know." He rubbed a soothing hand across her back. Her hair was wet against his cheek and smelled of something tropical. "You did everything right, though. And you saved your son." He felt her nod against his shoulder. "You were very brave."

She stilled then and sniffed as she pulled away. "I was, wasn't I?" Her watery eyes found his, testing his strength.

He cleared his throat. "If moms received medals, you'd be first in line."

Smiling, she said, "Just having my son here is reward enough." She stepped away then, breaking whatever connection they'd had. It was a connection he didn't want, but it had him wondering if he could overcome his fear and allow himself to love again.

Chapter Sixteen

Lily had, indeed, been brave yesterday. When Colton was in danger, she had gotten on a horse and she'd saved him. Question was, could she bring herself to ride again? In a normal, everyday setting, without the threat of losing one of her children propelling her into action, could she do it?

There was only one way to find out.

Having dropped Colton off at the ranch earlier and with Piper playing at Kenzie's, she pulled up to the stable, contemplating not only what she hoped to do today, but all that had transpired yesterday. Between almost losing her son and then being held in Noah's capable arms, savoring his warmth, drawing from his strength, she wasn't sure she'd ever be the same.

The memory of his embrace seemed to have taken up residence in her mind and had her thinking how nice it would be to have a companion. Someone to share life's joys and help bear the struggles. A safe place to land when things got tough.

Was she a fool to think of him as anything more than a friend?

Yes, yes, she was. Hadn't she already gone over that

with herself multiple times? Noah's actions were nothing more than those of a friend. Friends comforted each other.

But do friends whisper sweetly in your ear?

Why was she doing this to herself? Her children needed her. Yesterday had driven that point home, loud and clear. Besides, she'd be going back to Denver in a few weeks, so she might as well do herself a favor and keep her heart in check.

Especially since her little plan to test herself involved Noah's help.

She waited for the rain to let up before making a run for the stable. Unfortunately, the wet conditions meant any riding would have to be done in the stable, where Colton would likely see her.

Lily paused at the wooden door, watching drops of water fall sporadically from the overhang. What if she freaked out again? What if she couldn't do it?

I can do all things through Christ who strengthens me.

The verse from Philippians, chapter four, gave her hope. God had given her both the physical and emotional strength she'd needed to save Colton. Why would He stop now?

Inside, she shrugged out of her rain jacket and placed it on a hook just inside the office before seeking out Noah. She found him in the arena, still working with Colton on his roping skills. Perhaps she should have him teach her how to rope. That way, if she ever found herself in a situation similar to yesterday—which she had better not— she could simply lasso her children.

She waved as she passed, then continued on to see Honey.

The horse watched her as she approached, something Lily was getting used to. Not to mention the way the once-neglected animal seemed to stomp her feet, as though she was excited to see her.

"Good morning, my Honey girl." She slid the door aside. "How are you doing today?"

Honey nickered her response, a sound that never ceased to delight Lily. This once-neglected horse had come a long way in the past few weeks. She was actually starting to get some meat on her bones, which once seemed as though they might poke right through her skin. Her eyes shimmered, and she just seemed happy.

Retrieving the brush from the wall outside the stall, Lily swiped it over Honey's much-improved coat. "Does that feel good?"

The horse bobbed her head, making Lily chuckle.

"You're getting good at communicating with me."

"Lily?"

She turned at the sound of Noah's voice. "In here."

He placed a hand on either side of the stall's opening. "How's it going?"

"We're just enjoying a little rubdown." She continued to brush.

"No, I mean how are *you*?" He moved inside the stall. "Have you recovered from yesterday?"

"I think so. However—" her hands stilled, and she stepped back "—I need your help with something."

"Anything."

Her thumb ran across the bristles in her hand. "I need you to set me up with a horse."

"Set you up?"

"To ride. Or at least attempt to."

"Attempt? What about yesterday?" He stared down at her, confused.

"That's just it. I need to prove to myself that what happened yesterday wasn't a fluke. That I really can ride a horse without panicking."

"I get it." He crossed his arms over his chest. "You think you were only able to do it because of the circumstances."

"Exactly."

"Are you sure you're not overthinking this? You seemed pretty relaxed yesterday."

"That's why I need to find out." Her eyes drifted to the stall's dirt floor. "And I'd prefer Colton not see me."

"In case you fail."

Lifting her gaze, she nodded.

"Let me see what I can do." He left her then and, about fifteen minutes later, sent her a text message.

Colton is helping Dad in the barn. Meet me in the arena.

With a deep breath, she gave Honey a final nose rub. "I'll let you know how it goes."

Approaching the arena, she saw Noah waiting for her with the same dappled gray horse he'd tried to get her to ride a couple of weeks ago. Checkers.

She closed her eyes. *I can do this.*

Noah smiled as she came alongside him. "You can do this, Lily. I know you can." His faith in her had her smiling back, albeit rather nervously.

He stepped away. "You know what to do. Don't talk yourself out of it."

Her mind rewound to yesterday. Knowing Duke was the only way for her to get to Colton had gotten her into the saddle the first time. After that, it was pure necessity.

And everything turned out fine.

The ride back had even been somewhat enjoyable. The three of them talking while they meandered along. Once her blood pressure returned to normal, Lily had realized horseback riding was kind of fun. From atop Duke, she'd had a better perspective. She could see things she wasn't able to see on the ground. Such as that abandoned calf.

She reached for Checkers's saddle. Shoved her foot in the stirrup and pulled herself up.

"How does that feel?" Noah watched her.

Good question. She waited for the panic to set in. The sweaty palms. The churning stomach.

Nothing.

"I...think I'm okay." She reached for the reins. Nudged the horse's sides with her heels.

Checkers started walking at a snail's pace.

"Nudge him again," Noah coaxed.

She did. Then she felt Noah's eyes on her all the way around the arena.

Pride swelled inside her. With God's help, she'd done it. She'd overcome her fear and was actually riding a horse.

She made another lap at an even faster clip. "Woo-hoo!"

After one more round, she and Checkers came to a stop beside Noah.

Hands slung low on his hips, he grinned up at her. "How was it?"

Where did she begin? "Freeing. Exhilarating. Amazing."

"So you enjoyed it."

"Very much."

He held out a hand as she dismounted. Then refused to let go once her feet were on the ground. "Do you have any idea how proud I am of you?"

She lifted a shoulder. "If it's even half as proud as I am of me..."

"I'm just sorry I can't take credit for helping you."

"What do you mean? You got Colton out of the way and readied the horse. You encouraged me."

"But you had the determination. You wanted to prove something to yourself, and you did." The feel of his fingers against hers, the intensity of his gaze… "I think you deserve a reward."

"A reward?"

Still holding her hand, he tugged her across the arena. "Yes, and I know just the thing." He led her from the stable into the new building. But unlike the last time she'd passed through the corridor that connected the two, the metal walls were now covered with the same rustic wood they'd used in the stable.

"When did you do this?" Not only did it warm the space, it visually tied the two buildings together.

No response. Instead, he continued up the corridor until it ended at the arena.

Her mouth dropped open. Though she'd been in there once before, the day she found Noah and Andrew arguing, she hadn't paid much attention. "This place is huge." She eyed the metal rafters that spanned the ceiling. This arena was double, maybe triple the size of the one in the stable.

He veered left, past a handful of stalls that were also new and lined with the same rough wood. Approaching the far end of the building, she saw the pens and chutes.

"Where are you taking me?" Couldn't he at least let her look around? Maybe give her a tour of new place?

Finally, he stopped beside something covered in a blue tarp and let go of her hand. "I was going to wait until later to show you this, but I think you deserve to see it now."

She couldn't imagine, but, "Okay."

"Close your eyes."

Her brow lifted.

Arms crossed, he stared down at her. "I'm not removing the tarp until you close your eyes."

"Oh, all right." She covered her eyes. "Satisfied?"

"Give me one minute."

The rustle of the tarp had curiosity mingling with excitement.

"Okay, you can look."

Lowering her hands, she waited for her eyes to adjust.

Staring at the red barrel-shaped thing with straps, she couldn't— She burst out laughing then, realizing what it was. "A mechanical bull?" She looked at him now. "But I thought you said they were an insult."

"No, comparing rodeo cowboys to the cowboy wannabes in *Urban Cowboy* was an insult. Besides, this isn't mechanical."

"It isn't?"

"No. See the handle back here?"

She twisted to see. "Oh. Sure enough."

"Are you ready to get on?"

"Me?"

Moving so close that she could smell the woodsy scent of his soap, he lowered his head until his mouth was right by her ear. "Come on, Lily. Don't you trust me?"

She couldn't help smiling as she looked up at him. The twinkle in his browner-than-brown eyes. The teasing tilt of his lips. She did trust him. Perhaps too much. Definitely more than she'd ever wanted or expected to. And no matter how hard she tried, she seemed powerless to resist.

One more interview and he was home free.

That was, unless Lily scheduled something else. Which wouldn't surprise Noah in the least. The woman was the best thing that ever could have happened to the rodeo school.

He could hardly believe that the grand opening was just a little over a month away. And, honestly, he wasn't sure he'd have been able to pull it off if God hadn't brought Lily into his life. Sure, he could have managed a cake and some balloons, a few tours of the facility. But Lily had created an entire event. One that was certain to draw people in and make sure everyone knew about The Rodeo School at Abundant Blessings Ranch.

"What are you grinning about?" His father eyed him over his cup of coffee Monday morning.

"I'm not grinning." Sitting on the opposite side of the table in the ranch house kitchen, he sipped his own brew as the first rays of sunlight appeared outside the window over the sink. Lord willing, they'd have another dry day, making it two in a row.

"All right, then something's got you *smiling*."

"Just thinking about the rodeo school."

"The rodeo school or the woman helping you with the rodeo school?" The old man shoved his last bite of toast into his mouth.

"Dad…" Could he not just drink his coffee in peace? He rested his forearms on the wooden tabletop, eager to turn the tables. "I haven't seen Hillary around much lately."

"Her daughter, Celeste, has had some pretty bad morning sickness, so Hillary's been helping out with her two girls and one-year-old boy. Not to mention making sure things are running smoothly over there at Granny's Kitchen."

"Sounds like she's got her hands full."

"She can handle it. The woman thrives in chaos." He stared into his mug, falling unusually silent for a long moment. "You know…you and me…" he met Noah's gaze, his brow creased. "We were blessed to have been loved by a couple of mighty fine women."

Noah leaned back, stretching his legs out in front of him, uncertain where Dad was going with this conversation. "Can't argue with you there. Mama and Jaycee were the cream of the crop."

Dad shifted in his seat, tilting his cup one way and then the other, looking intently at whatever was left inside. "Lately, God's been showing me that there are other good women out there that need the love of a good man. I reckon that's why I've been spending so much time with Hillary."

Noah drew his legs back as he sat up straight. "Dad, are you thinking about getting married again?"

The old man held up a hand. "Now let's not go jumpin' the gun. All I'm sayin' is that I'm starting to realize that my feelings for Hillary are more than just…friendly."

Man, did he understand that. Better than he ever thought he would. Envisioning Lily as more than a friend seemed to be getting easier by the day.

"Do you think Hillary feels the same way?"

"I can't say for certain, but I believe so. She's very cautious when it comes to matters of the heart." He looked right at Noah. "Her ex-husband left her for another woman when Celeste was just a little girl. And I expect it left a pretty big scar."

"Humph." Noah's grip tightened around his mug until he feared he might break it. He eased up. "Wade Davis cheated on Lily."

"Your mama always said that women who've been betrayed like that have a lot of love to give. They're just afraid to give it for fear they'll get hurt again." Dad stood and moved to the coffeepot beside the sink to refill his cup. "I expect Lily's one of those women. The way she dotes on those kids and that rescue horse. She's a keeper, all right."

She was that and more. "I'm not sure the rodeo school would be a reality without her."

His father returned to his seat. "Lily's a good woman. She deserves a good man. And those kids…" Steam rose from his cup. "They need someone they can look up to."

Noah raised his mug. "I agree. I just don't think I'm that man." No matter how much he'd allowed himself to think about it.

"I do."

A quick intake of breath had him choking on his drink. "How can you be so sure?"

"Because for the first time in ages, you're happy—I mean genuinely happy. And it's got nothing to do with the horses or the rodeo school. It's because of Lily and her kids."

"And in case you've forgotten, they live in Denver." Ready for this conversation to be over, Noah shoved away from the table. "I've got an interview to get ready for." He went to his room down the hall and grabbed a fresh shirt for the interview, as well as another pair of boots before heading down to the stable.

Dad was falling in love with Hillary. Noah supposed he shouldn't be too surprised. Since the two former schoolmates had reconnected a year and half ago, they'd spent a good bit of time together. It was nice to see the old man getting out again.

Yet the notion of his father remarrying had never crossed his mind. It was hard to imagine him with anyone but Mama. Still, Hillary seemed to fit right in. She certainly knew how to keep his father in line. Yet despite their banter, there were little things Noah had noticed that

said she cared about Dad. Like the way she looked at him.
As though he was the most important person in the world.

But loving posed the risk of losing. Noah had experienced both. He'd lost his wife, child and mother. He wasn't
sure he could go through that again.

He unlocked the front door to the stable and flipped on
the lobby light as he entered. Just as he'd done every other
day for the past two and half years. And then he'd usually stay until well after dark. That was, until he met Lily.

Tucking his fear aside for a moment, he allowed himself to wonder what it would be like to have someone to
come home to. Someone to talk to other than his father or
brothers. Someone to discuss his day with and take just
as much interest in theirs. It had been so long since he'd
had that, he'd all but forgotten.

He thought about all of Lily's ideas for the rodeo school
and grand opening. They made a good team. And the
kids... Colton and Piper were great. Colton had grown
so much. In the short time he'd been here, he'd gone from
being a smart-mouthed kid too eager to grow up to a
respectful, happy-go-lucky boy truly experiencing his
childhood.

After depositing his shirt and boots in the office, he
roughed a hand over his face. He needed to stop thinking
and get to work. Otherwise he'd only succeed in driving
himself crazy.

He eyed his watch and went to check on the horses. His
hired hands would be here soon, and he hoped he'd have
at least one more opportunity to go over things with Lily
before the reporter arrived at eleven. Of course, she'd tell
him he already knew the answers to whatever they might
ask him and then tell him to speak from his heart, but he
still worried he might put his foot in his mouth.

His phone vibrated in his pocket as he approached

Honey's stall. His heart beat faster when he pulled it out to see Lily's name on the screen.

He pressed the button. "Good morning."

"Morning." She sounded tired.

"You all right?"

She yawned. "I was up with Piper most of the night. Poor kid's got some sort of stomach bug."

"Is she okay?"

"She will be once whatever it is runs its course." She blew out a breath, and he could picture her running her fingers through her long waves. "Things seem to have settled in the last couple of hours. She's asleep now, so that's a good sign. However, I'm afraid I won't be able to make it out there today."

"No, of course not." He toed at the dirt. "Piper needs you."

"Thank you for understanding. I just pray that neither Colton nor I will catch it. Or you, for that matter."

"No, I'm sure I'll be fine. You just concentrate on Piper."

"Call me after the interview. I want to know how it goes."

"I will." Tugging open the door to Honey's stall, he added, "Tell Piper I hope she feels better. And if you need one of us to come get Colton, just let me know."

He ended the call and moved toward the horse, feeling more than a little conflicted.

How on earth was he going to get through this interview without Lily?

Chapter Seventeen

Lily felt bad that she hadn't been able to be there for Noah's interview yesterday. While she knew he was perfectly capable of doing it on his own, she also knew that he liked having her there for moral support. So, now that Piper was back to her usual bubbly self, Lily had invited Noah to dinner at their place tonight to, hopefully, make up for her absence. Or at least ease her conscience.

Standing in the kitchen, chopping tomatoes for a salad, she peered through the wall of windows overlooking the deck where Piper was coloring at the table while Colton practiced with the rope Noah had given him.

A few months ago, she never would have envisioned such a scene. Yet, there it was. Had her children ever been this content?

Their lives were so different here than they were back in Denver. There, the kids spent most of their time inside the house. In Ouray, they were almost always outside, living life and experiencing new things. Especially when they were at the ranch. From the animals to playing in the river to exploring… Those were memories they would cherish forever. And probably miss when they got back home.

No doubt about it, life was just better here. For her and the kids. Who would have thought that small-town life would fit her so well? Yet, here she felt more relaxed. Probably because she didn't have to worry about living up to someone else's expectations. She was free to be herself. Just Lily. She rinsed her hands, dreading the thought of returning to Denver in a couple of weeks. So much so that she'd even entertained the idea of moving to Ouray.

What was holding her back then? Aside from the custody arrangements with Wade and how impossible he could make such a move if he chose to.

She reached for a towel. Noah. Or more to the point, her growing feelings for him. What if those feelings weren't reciprocated? He was still in love with his late wife. Was he capable of loving someone else?

"Noah's here." Colton rushed through the living room to the front door with his sister on his heels.

They must have seen his truck pull up.

She hurried into the bathroom, finger combed her hair and added a swipe of lip balm.

Why are you primping? It's not like this is a date.

Eyeing herself in the mirror, she frowned. "Oh, be quiet."

Both kids were clamoring for Noah's attention by the time she got to the door. At least she was pretty sure it was Noah. This wasn't the cowboy she was used to seeing. He wore a pair of stone-colored shorts and a blue button-down shirt with the sleeves rolled up to the elbows. His cowboy boots had been replaced by flip-flops, and there wasn't a cowboy hat in sight. Instead, his thick dark hair looked slightly damp, as though he'd just showered.

Making her wish she'd primped a little more.

"Look at the picture I made for you." Piper waved the

paper in front of him. "It's a horse, and I colored him to look just like Duke. Want to color with me?"

"Come watch me practice," said Colton. "You can show me—"

"Hey, you two." Hands on her hips, she glared at her children. "Noah is our guest. He's here for dinner, not to entertain you."

Behind them, Noah shrugged. "It's okay. I really don't mind."

Her gaze drifted from him to the kids. "All right. But if you give them an inch, they'll take a mile."

"I'll consider myself warned. But first—" he moved toward her and held out a brown paper gift bag "—this is for you."

Wrapping her fingers around the handles, she simply blinked. "For me?" Her heart raced as his hand brushed hers.

"Ouray may not have any flower shops," he said, "but we do have some of the world's finest chocolate."

Her brow lifted as she peered inside. "Mouse's?"

"The one and only."

She lifted out a small box. "I love that place. And you're right. Their chocolate is amazing." She hugged the box to her chest. "Thank you."

"I like their cookies," said Colton.

"Their chocolate mice are my favorite." Piper rubbed her tummy and licked her lips. "They're yummy."

Lily looked at Noah. "I may have to hide these."

While he joined the kids on the deck, Lily pulled the homemade lasagna out of the oven, then put in the garlic bread to brown. She couldn't believe he'd brought her a gift. *And does he look amazing or what?*

She nudged the thought aside, grabbed plates and silverware, and went outside to set the table.

"I like this view." Noah leaned against the wooden railing. "The way it looks down on the town."

She moved beside him. "That's the main reason I chose it." Her gaze lifted to the Amphitheater, the grayish rock formation that curved around the eastern edge of the town. "Sometimes, after the sun sinks behind the mountains, but before it actually sets, it casts these incredible shades of rose, orange and purple over the Amphitheater."

"Alpenglow."

Her gaze moved to his. "What?"

"The colors. It's called alpenglow." He turned so his back was against the rail. "Some natural occurrence having to do with particles in the air."

"Whatever it is, I absolutely love it."

Midway through the peach cobbler she'd made, the conversation turned to business, and Colton and Piper made themselves scarce while she and Noah lingered over coffee.

"This is just a random thought." She set her cup on the metal tabletop. "Something to think about for the future." Twisting toward him, she continued, "But have you ever thought of adding summer camps to the mix? Like two- or three-week-long rodeo camps where people from just about anywhere, looking to hone their skills, could come and train and immerse themselves in rodeo." She shrugged. "Of course, you'd have to provide room and board for something like that. Still, it would be an opportunity to reach people beyond this region."

"I'd never thought of that, but it's not a bad idea." He sat up straighter. "It would definitely be an opportunity to expand the school." He grew quiet then. Contemplative. "I really appreciate it when you throw out ideas like that."

"You do?"

"You have a fresh perspective that challenges me." His hand covered hers. "I like that."

"Mom?"

She turned to see Colton poking his head out of the door.

"Piper's asleep."

"Okay. I'll get her." She picked up her plate as she stood. "You need to get ready for bed, too, Colton. You have an early day tomorrow."

"Yes, ma'am."

Noah reached for her plate. "I'll take care of the dishes. You go take care of Piper."

Gratitude filled her as her gaze drifted to his. "Thank you."

His smile warmed her, but not nearly as much as the look she saw in his deep brown eyes. A look she'd not seen before. One of longing. Hope.

She stepped away for fear he'd be able to hear her heart pounding. "I won't be long."

After settling Piper, Lily went to check on Colton. He was already in bed, his wilderness comforter pulled up to his neck.

"Mom, do we have to go back to Denver?"

She eased beside him, wishing she could say, "No, of course not," but decided to play the adult instead. "Well, it's where our home is. Your school. Friends."

Lying on his back, he lifted a shoulder. "We could get a house here. I've seen lots of them for sale."

"What about your friends?"

"I can make new ones. And I already have one friend."

"Who's that?"

"Megan."

"Oh, yes." She adjusted his covers, amazed at how his thoughts mirrored her own. "What about your father?"

Colton was quiet for a moment. "It's not like we ever see him. Even when we do go to his house, he's hardly ever there."

A pattern Wade wasn't likely to change.

Smiling down at her boy, she brushed the hair off his forehead. "Moving is a big decision. One I can't make without praying about it, because a lot of things would have to fall into place." Such as custody issues.

His green eyes filled with hope. "Will you? Pray about it, I mean?"

She pondered his words. While she'd hoped and wished, she had yet to pray. Something she really ought to do. "I will."

"Promise?"

"Pinkie promise." She held up her little finger.

He hooked his to it and squeezed. "Thanks, Mom." Sitting up, he hugged her.

She kissed his cheek. "Good night, sweetie."

Returning to the main part of the house, she found the kitchen void of any dishes and Noah again on the deck. "Sorry I took so long." She joined him at the railing, taking in the multitude of stars twinkling in the sky as the cool air whispered over her arms.

"Everything all right?"

"Yes. Just a little…strange."

"How so?" Keeping one elbow on the rail, he faced her.

"Maybe *strange* isn't the right word. More like *unexpected*." She met Noah's gaze. "Colton asked me if we had to go back to Denver. Seems he'd be just as content to stay in Ouray."

"And what about you?"

She again studied the stars. "I've been happier here than I've been in a long time. It's as though we were just existing in Denver. But here…we're alive."

He stroked her arm with the backs of his fingers. "I know what you mean. I've felt a lot more alive since you've been here, too."

Her heart cartwheeled in her chest. Looking up at him, she swallowed hard. "You have?"

Straightening, he cupped her cheek with his hand as he threaded his fingers into her hair and leaned toward her.

Closing her eyes, she drew in a deep breath, anticipating his kiss. He smelled of coffee and fresh air. Then his lips met hers, and possibly for the first time in her life, she thought she might swoon.

His arms found their way to her waist, and he pulled her closer, deepening their kiss. This was too good to be true. He wanted her to stay in Ouray. Wanted to—

He abruptly pulled away, leaving her lost in a romantic haze.

She opened her eyes as he released her.

His face was marred with confusion and pain. "I'm sorry, Lily. I can't do this." With that, he whisked past her and into the house.

She turned around just in time to see the front door close. *What just happened?*

Touching her fingers to her still-throbbing lips, she wandered into the house and dropped onto the sofa, her heart breaking as she struggled for answers.

One thing was obvious. Noah didn't want her.

So why did she still want him?

Her cell phone rang in the kitchen. Like a fool, she hoped it might be him and hurried to grab it. Instead, her attorney's name appeared on the screen. Why would he call her so late?

She shook her head to clear the fog from her brain before answering. "Geoffrey?"

"Lily, if you're not sitting down, I'd advise that you do so now."

That was rather cryptic. "Why? Is there a problem?"

"You could say that."

She racked her brain trying to comprehend what he was saying. "Go on."

"Wade is suing for full custody of Colton and Piper."

"Wait, what?" Since when was Wade interested in being a father?

"There's a photo that has surfaced showing Colton on the ground, as though he was bucked from a horse."

"Bucked from a horse? That never happened."

"I'm afraid it gets worse, Lily. Wade is claiming that you're an unfit mother. That you've put the children in danger, so he wants immediate custody and has managed to secure a preliminary hearing for Friday."

She rubbed a hand over her forehead and through her hair. "That's only three days from now."

"I know. Which is why I'm going to suggest you come back to Denver as soon as possible so we can go over things. Just let me know when, and I'll clear my schedule."

When the call ended, Lily staggered to the couch, her body shaking. Why was this happening? First Noah, now this. If she lost her kids…

A sob caught in her throat.

Her world was falling apart.

Noah was a fool.

How could he think about having a relationship with Lily when had yet to say goodbye to Jaycee? Yet, he'd kissed Lily, anyway. Then left without so much as an explanation.

Pulling up to the ranch house, he contemplated turning around and going back. But he wasn't sure he could face Lily until his conscience was clear.

Inside the house, he barely spoke to his father as he passed through the living room. Once in his room, he opened the top drawer of his dresser and pulled out the note his mother had written to him shortly before she passed away. A note he hadn't even known existed until last year. Instead, it had been tucked away until his sister-in-law Carly stumbled across it.

He sat on the edge of his bed, opened the card with a columbine on the front and read.

My dearest Noah,
The first time I held you in my arms, I knew I was created to be a mother. You were my sunshine on cloudy days, always quick with a smile. But that smile faded when Jaycee died. As though a part of you had died with her.

You were a good husband. You loved Jaycee with everything you had. Though that doesn't mean you can't love again.

Your loyalty is one of your greatest traits, but, someday, God may bring a woman into your life who makes you smile once more and infiltrates your thoughts at the most unexpected times.

He looked up. Even Dad had said it was nice to see him happy again. Was it really because of Lily? She definitely seemed to find her way into his mind on a daily basis. Morning, noon and night. He was helpless to stop it. Perhaps because he didn't want to.

He continued to read.

Allowing yourself to love her won't mean you love Jaycee any less. You just have to let go of the past.

Weeping may endure for a night, but joy cometh in the morning. You deserve joy, my son. So much joy.

When he'd first read this letter a little over a year ago, he'd been touched by his mother's sentiment. Now her words smacked him in the face. She was right. It was time to let go of the past.

But how?

He tossed and turned most of the night until just before dawn. Then, as though a bolt of lightning had struck him, he knew just what he needed to do. Something he'd put off for twelve years.

He gathered a few clothes and some canned goods from the pantry and wrote a note to his father, explaining that he was going to the cabin, asking him to cover things at the stable and begging him not to let anyone know where he was. He set it beside the coffee maker before heading out the door.

The road to the cabin was overgrown, barely wide enough for his truck to get through anymore. Something he'd need to remedy.

When he reached the cabin, he stepped out of the cab, allowing the sun's rays to warm him as he stared at the abandoned house. When he'd first left, shortly after Jaycee's death, his mother had taken care of it. Until she got sick. Since then, Dad checked on it occasionally, making sure there were no major issues.

Noah wasn't sure how long he stood there, remembering the life he and Jaycee had built here. The dreams they shared and looked forward to expectantly. Dreams that came to an abrupt end the day she died. But the memories they'd made here remained. Good memories that he'd all but forgotten because he'd allowed them to be overshadowed by the bad.

That had to stop.

After turning on the power to the house, he made his way up the steps and onto the wooden porch. It was still solid, though it could use a good power washing and another coat of stain.

He drew in a deep breath as he unlocked the door and stepped inside. The room was dark and smelled musty. Shoving aside the curtains on either side of the door, he opened the windows, allowing the fresh air to flow in.

Funny, the living room was much smaller than he remembered. Though it looked just the way it had the day he walked in and found Jaycee lying on the floor.

A lump formed in his throat, but he swallowed it away. The last time he was in here, he'd taken only what was his and left everything that reminded him of her behind. As though not being surrounded by Jaycee's things could diminish her memory.

Moving past the leather sofa, he picked up a framed wedding photo from the bookshelf, recalling how excited he'd been to make Jaycee his wife. It wasn't long after that he'd made the decision to leave the rodeo and come back here to start a family. So many plans. Plans that died right along with Jaycee.

For years he'd begged God to take him, too. Every time he got on the back of a bronc or bull. Until he finally realized that, maybe, God still had him here for a reason. That's when the idea for the rodeo school first took root.

God, thank You for bringing Jaycee into my life, even if it was only for a short time. She taught me what it meant to love.

He continued through the house, opening curtains and windows, flooding the space with sunlight. Light that revealed the signs of neglect. How could he do that to Jaycee's memory?

Well, not anymore.

He rolled up the sleeves of his work shirt and went outside. After locating a pair of trimming shears in the shed out back, he attacked the overgrown lilac bush and brought it under control. Next, he brushed away cobwebs from the outside of the house and cleaned the windows, removing twelve years' worth of haze.

Inside, he moved from room to room, wiping down walls, dusting, scrubbing floors and vacuuming. After making sure the washer and dryer were still in working order, he stripped linens from beds and took down dust-laden curtains.

The sun was setting when he finally sat down on the porch with a bowl of canned chili. The once-forgotten cabin looked more like a home now. A place Jaycee would be proud of.

A place he actually wanted to be.

Waking up in the cabin the next morning, Noah felt like a new man. Good thing he'd hung on to that container of coffee he found in the cupboard yesterday.

Lifting his cup, he took another sip. A little on the stale side, but it would do.

He wandered through the house, thoughts of Lily peppering his brain. What was she doing? Had she brought the kids out for lessons? Had she come to check on Honey? He should have called her, told her what he was doing.

After locating a box in one of the closets, he gathered all of the photos around the house and placed them in it. He didn't need them to remind him of Jaycee. She would live in his heart forever. But it was time for him to move forward.

Standing in the hallway, he studied the two second-ary bedrooms. Why were they so small? Okay for a baby or small child, he supposed, but Colton and Piper would need more space. Peering into the so-called master, he realized that it wasn't much better, except that it had its own bathroom. He couldn't expect Lily to live—

A smile split wide across his face when he realized what he was contemplating. And for the first time in twelve years, he felt his heart truly beat. A pounding, strong and vibrant, as though it had finally broken free of the grief that had held it captive.

He fell against the wall. "I love her. I love Lily." Why had it taken him so long to realize it? "God, I don't know how, but I have to make this right."

He rushed outside to his truck. He had to find Lily.

It was just after noon when he reached the ranch house and burst through the mudroom door.

"Dad?"

"Noah, just the person I need to see." Carly met him as he moved from the mudroom into the family room.

"I can't talk right now." He moved past her. "I need to find Lily."

"You're going to Denver?"

His steps slowed. He turned to face her. "What are you talking about? She's in town."

"No, Lily left for Denver yesterday." Carly reached for a stack of papers on the end table beside the sofa. "She asked me to give you these flyers for the grand opening."

"Denver?" He sank onto the couch. Why would she go back now?

"Yeah." Carly set the papers back down again. "She seemed pretty upset, too."

He buried his face in his hands. *Because of me.*

"Noah!" Dad rushed in from the adjoining kitchen. "Lily's on TV." Remote already in hand, the old man turned up the volume.

Looking at screen on the other side of the room, Noah saw side-by-side photos of Lily and her ex-husband.

"Billionaire businessman-turned-state-senate candidate Wade Davis is suing for custody of his two children after a photo surfaced earlier this summer, showing his son grimacing in pain after being bucked from a horse," the announcer said.

Standing, Noah stared at the image on the screen. "I remember that. He wasn't bucked off. He tripped and fell."

"And came up laughing, as I recall," said Dad.

"Davis appeared before reporters—" the announcer continued as they cut to a clip of Wade Davis.

"The welfare of my children is my top priority. I cannot risk having them put in danger."

"Danger?" Noah started to pace. "This guy is out of his mind."

A picture of Lily flashed on the screen as the announcer again spoke. "The children's mother, Lily Davis, daughter of late real estate mogul Gunther Yates, refused comment. The former darlings of Denver are due in court tomorrow."

He turned away. Lily had trusted him, and he'd let her down. *Why did I have to walk away?*

Dad came alongside him. "What are you going to do now?"

Chapter Eighteen

Lily sat at the front of a Denver courtroom Friday morning with her attorney by her side as they awaited the judge's arrival. Across the aisle, at a duplicate table, her ex-husband eyed her smugly.

He hadn't changed. This lawsuit had nothing to with being a father. It was about his political campaign and appearances. He thought that if he played the doting father, it would garner him more votes. Lily was certain of it.

Her stomach churned. Her only defense was the truth. She'd done nothing wrong. That photo they were trying to use against her, to prove her an unfit mother, was a lie. Something taken completely out of context. And if needed, she had witnesses who would confirm that.

Still, Wade's self-satisfied grin rubbed her the wrong way.

Standing, she crossed to where he sat. "Why are you doing this, Wade? You know I would never put my children in danger, just like you know that picture doesn't portray the real story." Arms crossed, she cocked her head. "How did you get it, anyway? Did the photographer offer it to you? Was he looking to pad his wallet?"

Wade leaned back in his chair, one side of his mouth

lifting in amusement. "You seem awfully worried, Lily. Is there something you'd care to tell me?"

Anger sparked inside her, but she tamped it down, unwilling to give him the satisfaction.

Out of the corner of her eye, she saw the doors open at the back of the courtroom. Corrine Davis, Wade's current wife and Lily's former best friend, walked in. The woman Lily had once been foolish enough to share all of her secrets with was as beautiful as ever in her perfectly tailored navy pantsuit, though her shoulder-length hair was a shade blonder than Lily remembered.

With a final look at Wade, Lily returned to her seat, not wanting to cause a scene.

Corrine paused beside her husband, almost glaring at him, then continued around that table toward Lily.

Her heart beat faster. What could Corrine possibly have to say to her? Would she call Lily an unfit mother and pretend to care for Colton and Piper as if they were her own?

Stopping in front of their table, she nodded in Lily's direction before pulling a plain manila file folder from her leather Salvatore Ferragamo tote and handing it to Lily's lawyer. "This is for you."

Her gaze moved to Lily. "I'm sorry, Lily. For everything." With that, Corrine turned on her Jimmy Choo heel and moved across the granite floor, past Wade and his attorney, back down the aisle and out the door.

Weird.

Lily leaned toward her attorney. "What did she give you?"

Only then did Geoffrey open the file just enough for him to peer inside.

"Well…?" She waited anxiously.

He straightened. Then sent her a smile. "Excuse me, please."

She watched as he stood and made his way to the other table. What was going on? And why wasn't Geoffrey sharing anything with her? He did work for her, after all.

"Some information has come to light that you two might be interested in." He handed the folder to Wade's attorney.

The man opened it so that both he and his client could see its contents.

Yet, she was being kept in the dark.

The lawyer riffled through the papers, and Wade's eyes went wide. Wade and his attorney exchanged looks. Then he slumped back into his chair, a scowl on his face as his attorney closed the folder and handed it back to Geoffrey.

Lily's lawyer returned to her side as the judge entered the courtroom.

"All rise for the honorable Judge Rawlings."

Standing, Lily leaned toward Geoffrey and whispered, "What's going on?"

The judge gaveled in. "You may be seated." The older, fatherly-looking man took his seat behind the bench.

Geoffrey grinned. "Let's just say that a leopard doesn't change his spots," he whispered.

"What?" All of these ambiguities were about to drive her crazy.

"First order of business, Davis versus Davis," said the judge.

Wade's lawyer stood. "Your Honor, counsel requests permission to approach the bench."

"Permission granted."

Wade's attorney moved forward and spoke to the judge in hushed tones.

The suspense was killing her.

A few moments later, Wade's attorney returned to his seat as the judge gaveled once again.

"The case of Davis versus Davis has been dismissed."

Now Lily was really confused, and she couldn't help but wonder what her ex-husband was up to now.

"Dismissed? Geoffrey?" Standing, she watched as he gathered his papers.

Finally, he met her gaze. "Corrine is filing for divorce."

Lily didn't think it was possible, but she found herself even more puzzled. "Why?"

"Let's just say there was a third party involved. And some photos confirmed it."

"A third— Oh. Oh…" So Wade was cheating on Corrine. Now it all made sense. The dismissal, Corrine's apology.

Despite everything, though, she felt sorry for her old friend. The sting of betrayal hurt on many levels.

Again, she eyed her ex-husband across the aisle, a new sense of determination flooding through her. The more she discovered about this man, the more she felt the need to protect her children from his self-serving antics. And protect them she would.

She approached him once more. "That didn't turn out so well for you, did it, Wade?" Laying her hands atop the table, she leaned toward him. "Well, it's about to get worse, because not only will I be seeking full custody of my children, I can assure you that I will receive it."

Moments later, with Geoffrey at her side, Lily exited into the large granite lobby and blew out a breath. *Thank You, Lord.* Not only had He vindicated her, He seemed to be paving the way for her and her children to live the life they'd been praying for.

She faced her attorney. "Thank you for everything, Geoffrey. I appreciate—"

"Lily."

Her pulse raced. It couldn't be.

She turned to find Noah standing behind her with his cowboy hat in hand. He wore a pair of dark-wash jeans, ostrich boots and a slate blue polo shirt that highlighted his dark eyes every bit as much as his bulging biceps.

She swallowed hard. "What are you— How did you know I was here?"

"Carly said you'd gone back to Denver. The news report said you were due in court today." He shrugged. "I took my chances, because I couldn't let you go through this alone."

Her mind still reeling, she said, "That—that's sweet." She rubbed her temple. "Noah, this is my attorney, Geoffrey Forester. Geoffrey, Noah Stephens."

While they shook hands and exchanged pleasantries, Lily tried to gather her thoughts.

Geoffrey touched her elbow. "I'll leave you two alone."

She nodded. "Thank you, Geoffrey."

"Are you okay?" Noah watched her as Geoffrey strode away. "You don't look so good."

"Yes, I'm fine. Just a little overwhelmed." Could this day possibly get any crazier?

"Here, let's sit down." He gestured to a wooden bench along the wall. "How'd it go in there?"

She lifted a shoulder. "It was over before it began." She told him all that had transpired and that the case had been dismissed.

"That's excellent news."

"Yes, it is." She dared to meet his gorgeous dark gaze. "What are you doing here? I mean, if you're feeling guilty about the other night, it's okay, I get it. You didn't have to come all the way to Denver."

"I did feel guilty, but not for the reasons you might think."

She cocked her head, daring to hope as she waited for him to continue.

"I love you, Lily. Of that I couldn't be more certain."

Tears of joy pricked the backs of her eyes.

"But I wasn't free to tell you until I'd let go of the past."

Finding her voice, she said, "Your steadfast love for Jaycee is one of the things I admire most about you."

"I never thought I'd love again, Lily. Until I met you." He took hold of her hand. "You are my future. You, Colton and Piper." Reaching into his pocket, he pulled out a velvet box and dropped to one knee. "Please say that you'll marry me."

Oh, boy, things had just gotten crazier.

"I'm willing to forgo the rodeo school and live in Denver until the children graduate from high school. I just want to be with you."

She touched a hand to his cheek. "The fact that you'd postpone your dream makes me love you all the more."

He smiled up at her.

"But the kids and I have already decided that we want to make Ouray our home." She shrugged. "I'll have to tie up some loose ends here, but, Lord willing, we'll be there in time for the kids to start school."

"Well, I know of a nice little cabin, just outside Ouray. You and the kids are more than welcome to stay there."

The joy in her heart spilled into a smile. "I'd like that, but we should discuss this marriage thing with the kids before I give you an answer." Her cheeks heated. "Although I'm pretty sure I know what they're going to say."

"In that case..." Standing, he tugged her to her feet, gazing down at her as though she was the most special person in the world.

She pressed a hand against his chest. "I love you, Noah."

"I love you, too. With all of my heart." As he smiled down at her, she pushed up on the toes of her pumps and kissed him without reservation. This was the man she'd longed for. And even though she'd given up on her dream of true love, God had fulfilled it, bigger and better than she ever could have imagined.

"Here's to Noah and a successful grand opening." Dad lifted his cup of lemonade.

"Hear, hear," echoed the rest of the family lining the deck on the Saturday evening of Labor Day weekend.

Noah wrapped an arm around Lily's shoulders and pulled her close. "None of this would have been possible without this woman by my side." He peered down at her, making her heart flutter. Hard to believe that in just a little over a month, she would be his wife. She could hardly wait.

Wade had not contested her petition for full custody of the children, though she had agreed to grant him visitation. He'd also decided to pull out of the race for state senate. Given all that had transpired in his personal life over the past few weeks, his polling numbers had dropped significantly. Lily prayed he might use this time to reevaluate his life and his choices and turn over a new leaf.

"Lily," Noah continued, "you took a grand opening that would have been mediocre at best and turned it into an event I never would have thought possible."

"Yeah," said Colton. "We might even be on TV." Thanks to a couple of reporters who'd shown up, referring to the grand opening as a not-to-be-missed event.

"Hey, great job with the calf roping out there, Colton." Jude patted him on the back.

Lily was so proud. The kid had ridden his heart out and hit the mark on his first try.

"I still can't believe how many people came." Andrew shook his head. "It was standing room only in there."

"Lily and I calculated somewhere in the neighborhood of

four to five hun…dred—" Seemingly perplexed, Carly laid a hand on her husband's arm. "I think my water just broke."

"What does that mean?" Colton's face contorted.

Clint moved toward his daughter-in-law. "It means these two had better get going, because they're about to have a baby."

"What do I do? Do we have enough time to make it to the hospital? Are you in pain?" Andrew's rapid-fire questions were accompanied by a look of terror. Understandable, Lily supposed. Since Megan wasn't his biological daughter, he'd never experienced the whole childbirth thing before.

"I'm fine," Carly assured him. "Though I don't know for how much longer, so yes, we should probably go to the hospital."

Andrew looked at his father.

"Well, don't just stand there gaping, boy. You heard the woman." Clint pointed toward their vehicle. "Get her to the hospital."

Megan hugged her mother. "I can't wait. My first camp-out *and* I'm going to be a big sister. All in the same night."

With Andrew and Carly on their way, Lily helped Lacie clean up the paper plates and plasticware from dinner, while Clint and Hillary gathered the kids for their big campout—which the two had planned a week or so ago and that probably signaled the next step in their relationship, considering Hillary's granddaughters, Cassidy and Emma, were among the campers. Daniel had helped them set up tents near the river earlier today and get the firepit ready. All they had to do now was show up.

Returning to the deck, Lily joined her fiancé while Lacie stood in front of her husband to watch the group.

"Just look at them," said Lacie. "They're going to have so much fun."

Matt wrapped his arms around his wife's waist. "I just

hope we don't get a phone call in the middle of the night to come and pick her up because she misses us."

Noah placed his mouth beside Lily's ear, sending shivers down her spine. "Care to take a ride with me?"

"Mmm...a sunset ride sounds delightful." Not to mention romantic.

After seeing the children off, they headed to the stable for Duke and Checkers.

"I can't wait until Honey is strong enough to be ridden." She climbed into her saddle. "Not that you're not a good horse, Checkers." She patted the animal's neck. "Where do you want to go?" She eyed her intended. "The cabin?"

Since returning to Ouray, she and the kids had been living in Noah's cabin. Something that was much more practical, considering they spent most of their time at the ranch. That was, when the kids weren't in school.

Of course, their new rural life had presented a few adventures. Such as the morning they woke up to find a coyote in the front yard. She'd had to convince Piper that it was not a dog and she could not play with it. Fortunately, it ran away.

"Actually, I have someplace else in mind." The spark in his dark eyes had her curious.

"You lead then." Holding on to the reins, she followed him the short distance through the pasture, beyond the barn, admiring the way he looked in the saddle.

"I've been thinking about your idea of summer camps."

"Really?" This was the first time he'd mentioned it.

"We're still talking a ways down the road, but what if we had at least one that was dedicated to kids struggling with grief or loss?"

"That's always been a part of your dream." And she'd seen the positive effect horses had on Colton.

"I know something like that would involve counselors

and such, but I think I'd like to explore the possibility." He smiled as they came into a small wooded area that had a natural clearing in its midst. "And speaking of possibilities." He looked her way. "What would you think about building a home here?" He eased off Duke before coming to help her down.

"Building? What about the cabin?"

"Lily, I love that cabin. But we both know that it's way too small for all of us. It's barely big enough for you and the kids. Once I move in, we'll be on top of each other. Not to mention as the kids get older."

"I suppose things are a little tight." And while she didn't want anything near as large as the monstrosity she'd shared with her ex-husband, a little extra space never hurt.

"It's closer to the stable and the rodeo school. And if you look through here—" he tugged her a few feet over and turned her just so "—we'd have a spectacular view."

Though the sunlight was dwindling, she could still make out the unmistakable silhouette. "Ouray. Mount Hayden's peak, anyway."

"That's it." He stepped away, gesturing. "We could do a big porch that wraps around the entire house."

"Could we have a log home?"

"If you like. One story or two?"

"Hmm… I suppose a two-story home would afford us a better view." She pointed toward town.

"Or just a two-story wall of windows on the front."

"Ooh, now that would be a view. And we'd need at least four bedrooms."

"For a guest room?"

She slowly lifted her gaze to his. "Or a nursery." She hadn't broached the subject of more children before, but she knew Noah would be an amazing father. Besides, she'd always hoped for more kids.

His Adam's apple bobbed as he blinked several times.

She reached for his hand. "How would you feel about that?"

"I…" He blew out a breath. "I'm not going to lie. It kind of scares me."

"Then we don't—"

"But I also think a baby—" Taking a step closer, he cupped her cheek, weaving his fingers into her hair. "Our baby—" he grinned "—would be pretty exciting, too."

She smiled up at the man who would soon be her husband. "Then let's pray about it and see what God has in store."

"Good idea." Lowering his head, he kissed her. Soft and tender…then he abruptly pulled away. "If it's a girl, we have to name her Joy."

She liked that, but— "Okay. Why?"

The way he stared at her made her feel cherished. Something she'd never felt before. His hands moved to her waist. "Because that's what you've given me, Lily. You, Colton and Piper have taught me to live again. And I'm so glad God brought you into my life." He pulled her to him. "I love you. Today. Tomorrow. And for the rest of our lives."

Once more, he pulled her into his embrace. A place where she was safe. Where she could be herself. And where just Lily was a perfect fit.

* * * * *

Look for the next book in the
Rocky Mountain Heroes series
by Mindy Obenhaus,
available September 2019
wherever Harlequin Love Inspired
books and ebooks are sold.

Dear Reader,

Sometimes life doesn't turn out the way we planned. Hearts are broken, dreams shattered...

Noah and Lily had both loved and lost. Sure, their circumstances were different, but the pain inflicted by those losses was the same. They were left to carve a new path for themselves, apart from the lives they'd once envisioned.

I hope you enjoyed watching these two fall in love as much as I did. When we first met Noah in *Their Ranch Reunion*, the first book in my Rocky Mountain Heroes series, I was intrigued. This bigger-than-life former rodeo champ had lost both his wife and unborn child. He was a wounded soul, yet despite his desire to join his wife, he recognized that God still had a purpose for him. A purpose that ultimately brought him and Lily together.

And I loved Lily. While she had more money than most of us could fathom, she was grounded and real. She loved her children and had a deep desire to impart the same Godly values to them that her grandmother had instilled in her when she was young.

Two brothers remain in this series. Jude and Daniel. I can't wait to see what God has in store for them. Whatever it is, we'll be heading back to Ouray again to take in the beauty and charm of this unique little town.

In the meantime, I would love to hear from you. You can contact me via my website, mindyobenhaus.com, or you can snail-mail me c/o Love Inspired Books, 195 Broadway, 24th Floor, New York, NY 10007.

Until next time...
Mindy

A PERFECT AMISH MATCH
Indiana Amish Brides • by Vannetta Chapman

Positive he's meant to stay a bachelor, Noah Graber enlists Amish matchmaker Olivia Mae Miller to set up three dates—and prove to his parents that relationships aren't for him. But when he starts falling for Olivia Mae, can they forget their reasons for *not* marrying and build a future together?

HER NEW AMISH FAMILY
Amish Country Courtships • by Carrie Lighte

Widower Seth Helmuth needs a mother for his little twin boys, but for now, he hires the *Englischer* temporarily living next door as their nanny. But while he searches for the perfect wife and mother, he can't help but think Trina Smith is the best fit...if only she were Amish.

HIS WYOMING BABY BLESSING
Wyoming Cowboys • by Jill Kemerer

When pregnant widow Kit McAllistor arrives at Wade Croft's ranch hoping to stay in one of his cabins, Wade can't turn away his childhood best friend—even if his ranch may soon be for sale. But he's determined to keep his feelings for Kit and her baby strictly friendship.

HER TWINS' COWBOY DAD
Montana Twins • by Patricia Johns

Colt Hardin's surprised to learn his uncle's will is more complicated than he expected—he'll inherit the ranch he was promised...but his late cousin's twin toddlers get the cattle. Can he keep an emotional distance from the children's mother, Jane Marshall, until his purchase of the cattle is finalized?

THE RANCHER'S REDEMPTION
by Myra Johnson

Including his property in the local historical society's grand tour could have huge benefits for Kent Ritter, but he has no clue how to decorate it. So he strikes a deal with town newcomer Erin Dearborn—she'll give him decorating advice if he'll make repairs to her home.

RESTORING HER FAITH
by Jennifer Slattery

Hired to restore the town's church, artist Faith Nichols must work with widowed contractor Drake Owens on the project. But as they collaborate to renovate the building, will Faith restore Drake's heart, as well?

Get 4 FREE REWARDS!

We'll send you 2 FREE Books plus 2 FREE Mystery Gifts.

Love Inspired® books feature contemporary inspirational romances with Christian characters facing the challenges of life and love.

FREE Value Over $20

YES! Please send me 2 FREE Love Inspired® Romance novels and my 2 FREE mystery gifts (gifts are worth about $10 retail). After receiving them, if I don't wish to receive any more books, I can return the shipping statement marked "cancel." If I don't cancel, I will receive 6 brand-new novels every month and be billed just $5.24 for the regular-print edition or $5.74 each for the larger-print edition in the U.S., or $5.74 each for the regular-print edition or $6.24 each for the larger-print edition in Canada. That's a savings of at least 13% off the cover price. It's quite a bargain! Shipping and handling is just 50¢ per book in the U.S. and 75¢ per book in Canada.* I understand that accepting the 2 free books and gifts places me under no obligation to buy anything. I can always return a shipment and cancel at any time. The free books and gifts are mine to keep no matter what I decide.

Choose one: ☐ **Love Inspired® Romance Regular-Print**
(105/305 IDN GMY4)

☐ **Love Inspired® Romance Larger-Print**
(122/322 IDN GMY4)

Name (please print)

Address   Apt. #

City   State/Province   Zip/Postal Code

Mail to the **Reader Service:**
IN U.S.A.: P.O. Box 1341, Buffalo, NY 14240-8531
IN CANADA: P.O. Box 603, Fort Erie, Ontario L2A 5X3

Want to try 2 free books from another series? Call 1-800-873-8635 or visit www.ReaderService.com.

---

*Terms and prices subject to change without notice. Prices do not include sales taxes, which will be charged (if applicable) based on your state or country of residence. Canadian residents will be charged applicable taxes. Offer not valid in Quebec. This offer is limited to one order per household. Books received may not be as shown. Not valid for current subscribers to Love Inspired Romance books. All orders subject to approval. Credit or debit balances in a customer's account(s) may be offset by any other outstanding balance owed by or to the customer. Please allow 4 to 6 weeks for delivery. Offer available while quantities last.

Your Privacy—The Reader Service is committed to protecting your privacy. Our Privacy Policy is available online at www.ReaderService.com or upon request from the Reader Service. We make a portion of our mailing list available to reputable third parties that offer products we believe may interest you. If you prefer that we not exchange your name with third parties, or if you wish to clarify or modify your communication preferences, please visit us at www.ReaderService.com/consumerschoice or write to us at Reader Service Preference Service, P.O. Box 9062, Buffalo, NY 14240-9062. Include your complete name and address.

LI19R

"Dating is so complicated."

"People are complicated, Noah. Every single person you meet is dealing with something."

He asked, "How did you get so wise?"

"Never said I was."

"I'm being serious. How did you learn to navigate so seamlessly through these kinds of interactions, and why aren't you married?"

Olivia Mae thought her eyes were going to pop out of her head. "Did you really just ask me that?"

"I did."

"A little intrusive."

"Meaning you don't want to answer?"

"Meaning it's none of your business."

"Fair enough, though it's like asking a horse salesman why he doesn't own a horse."

"My family situation is…unique."

"You mean with your grandparents?"

She nodded instead of answering.

"I've got it." Noah resettled his hat, looking quite pleased with himself.

"Got what?"

"The solution to my dating disasters."

He leaned forward, close enough that she could smell the shampoo he'd used that morning.

"You need to give me dating lessons."

"What do you mean?"

"You and me. We'll go on a few dates…say, three. You can learn how to do anything if you do it three times."

"That's a ridiculous suggestion."

"Why? I learn better from doing."

"Do you?"

"I've already learned not to take a girl to a gas station, but who knows how many more dating traps are waiting for me."

"So this would be…a learning experience."

"It's a perfect solution." He tugged on her *kapp* string, something no one had done to her since she'd been a young teen.

"I can tell by the shock on your face that I've made you uncomfortable. It's a *gut* idea, though. We'd keep it businesslike—nothing personal."

Olivia Mae had no idea why the thought of sitting through three dates with Noah Graber made her stomach twirl like she'd been on a merry-go-round. Maybe she was catching a stomach bug.

"Wait a minute. Are you trying to get out of your third date? Because you promised your *mamm* that you would give this thing three solid attempts."

"And I'll keep my word on that," Noah assured her. "After you've tutored me, you can throw another poor unsuspecting girl my way."

Olivia Mae stood, brushed off the back of her dress and pointed a finger at Noah, who still sat in the grass as if he didn't have a care in the world.

"All right. I'll do it."

Don't miss
A Perfect Amish Match *by Vannetta Chapman,*
available May 2019 wherever
Love Inspired® books and ebooks are sold.

www.LoveInspired.com

LIEXP0419